Heart Flesh Degeneration

Studies in Austrian Literature, Culture, and Thought
Translation Series

General Editors:

Jorun B. Johns
Richard H. Lawson

Ludwig Laher

Heart Flesh Degeneration

A Novel

Afterword by Florian Schwanninger

Translated by Susan Tebbutt

Ariadne Press

Riverside, California

Ariadne Press would like to express its appreciation to the Bundeskanzleramt – Sektion Kunst, Vienna for assistance in publishing this book

.KUNST

Translated from the German *Herzfleischentartung*
© Haymon Verlag, Innsbruck-Wien 2001

Library of Congress Cataloging-in-Publication Data

Laher, Ludwig, 1955-
[Herzfleischentartung. English]
Heart flesh degeneration ; novel / Ludwig Laher ; afterword by Florian Schwanninger, translated by Susan Tebbutt
      p. cm -- (Studies in Austrian literature, culture, and thought)
ISBN 1-57241-150-3
  1   World War, 1939-1945—Concentration camps—Austria—Salzburg—Fiction. 2. Romanies—Nazi persecution—Austria—Salzburg—Fiction. 3 World War, 1939-1945—Atrocities—Fiction I. Schwanninger, Florian, 1977- II. Tebbutt, Susan III Title.

PT2672.A35114713 2006
833'.912--dc22
                                         2006020544

Cover Design
Art Director: George McGinnis

Copyright ©2006
by Ariadne Press
270 Goins Court
Riverside, CA 92507

All rights reserved
No part of this publication may be reproduced or transmitted in any form or by any means without formal permission
Printed in the United States of America
ISBN 1-57241-150-3, 9781572411500
(trade paperback original)

Contents

Ludwig Laher
Heart Flesh Degeneration 1

Author's Note 163

Author's Postscript 166

Afterword
Historical Background
by Florian Schwanninger 173

Glossary

Anschluss – Annexation
DAF [Deutsche Arbeitsfront] – German Labor Front
Gauleiter – Head of Regional Administrative District
    (Supreme territorial or regional Nazi Party authority)
Gestapo – German Secret Police
NSDAP [Nationalsozialistische Deutsche Arbeiterpartei] –
    Nazi Party
NSKK – National Socialist Motor Transport Corps
Oberdonau – Upper Danube region
Ortsgruppe – Local Unit
Reichsbahn – State Railroad
SA [Sturmabteilung] – Storm Detachment; Storm Troopers
SS [Schutzstaffel] – Special police force originally founded as
    a bodyguard for Adolf Hitler
Ständestaat – Reorganized Austrian State (1934-1938)
UFA – Universe Film Company
Volksgenosse – Fellow countryman; racial comrade
Zigeuner – Gypsy
Zigeuner-Mischling – Gypsy half-caste

For Maria Daniel on her 66th birthday
and for Rudolf Haas on his 60th

> *I said a few words, among other things that it's not the Third Reich I'm in, but Austria.*
>
> Sebastian Riess, farm laborer (during interrogation as a witness on February 10, 1941, when asked why he was sent on August 11, 1940 to the Labor Education Camp in St. Pantaleon-Weyer)

I

Franz Kubinger is forty-five, non-denominational, married, childless, of good repute; he has completed his obligatory schooling, and one day in the year 1939 has a good idea. The industrious Franz has worked his way up to the rank of Regional Unit Leader of the German Labor Front and knows his Regional Chairman well. The name of the Regional Chairman of the GLF is August Eigruber, but he is generally known in his joint capacity as Gauleiter and soon-to-be Reich Governor in Oberdonau. But Kubinger also knows Eigruber's second-in-command well, a man by the name of Franz Stadlbauer. The acting Regional Chairman and the Gauleiter are men to be relied on, always open to good ideas.

Kubinger, a political idealist right from the start, lives in the city of Linz on the Danube, has been a card-carrying Nazi Party member since 1933, and owns a semi-detached house in one of the most scenic spots in romantic Salzkammergut. That's also where he'd most like to see his good idea become reality, but the experts from the River Rapids Management Scheme advise strongly against it. Untrained workmen couldn't tame the raging mountain river, they argue. That's completely out of the question. But they might just have something for him, a sort of alternative; the only snag is that it's so far away. Why not drain a more than useless piece of moorland? This way they'd be doing a big service to an outstanding District Party Group Leader of the NSDAP [Nazi Party], a mayor to boot, and chairman of the local Water Cooperative.

Franz's enthusiasm has its limits, but for the sake of the good idea he goes along with it. He then arranges for the Gauleiter and Reich Governor to send a letter to his

2

own good self, in which he learns to his great satisfaction that the labor force of each and every able-bodied worker must be deployed to fulfill diverse tasks in the war that has been thrust upon Franz Kubinger and August Eigruber. That's how it is, nods Franz. But, as could be expected, he's informed that some people have no desire whatsoever to cooperate and that those people are now being put into an institution, into the regional camp for the reluctant, work-shy, and antisocial. It's Franz's good idea. A Regional Representative for Labor Education is brought in to select camp inmates, admit them, look after their pedagogical needs, and, if necessary, release them again. Party Member Franz Kubinger is entrusted with these duties; it's written down there in black and white. Now all his wishes are finally fulfilled; now our Franz is master over life and death.

But being so far away from his cozy second home and having other time-consuming obligations, Kubinger doesn't want to get his own hands dirty. So it comes in extremely handy that he also happens to be a senior SA Major in the executive of the Alpenland Branch of the SA. That's why Franz makes his trusty comrade August Staudinger the Camp Director. The latter feels chronically underpaid in the Reich Labor Service, has a reputation for being exceptionally ambitious, and is therefore looking for a post offering greater responsibility. The twenty-seven-year-old originally trained as a butcher and, before Austria was integrated into Hitler's Reich, earned his keep from time to time as a farmhand, organized self-defense and drill exercises in the forest for like-minded souls, and in the name of the new powers-that-be arrested on day X, the 12th of March, 1938, among others, the mayor of the town where he lived, and the following day he arrested the District Police Inspector of the town where he was born. He seems thus to be extremely well qualified in pedagogical terms to do Franz Kubinger's unambiguous tasks.

In the regional capital of Linz, both men are soon talking seriously about organizational matters. As Franz explains very candidly to August, they are admitting only people who are worthless. It might therefore be necessary on occasion to tie them to trees and give them a good thrashing. Would I be covered? asks August cautiously. Yes, says Franz. But he couldn't possibly have to assume responsibility if someone were to die in the process, could he, asks August. It's all covered, Franz assures him.

The compulsory dissolution of the trade unions meant the hour had come for the German Labor Front to be born. It assembles under its broad wings the Third Reich's employers and employees in industry, trade, and commerce, and does its ideological best to increase productivity. Membership in the Labor Front is, naturally, just as much voluntary as it is obligatory. The difference between the interests of the employers and those of the employees has thus been eradicated once and for all. And if anyone doesn't believe that, people like Franz Kubinger have come up with any number of good ideas for dealing with them.

Karl Gumpelmaier, for example, doesn't like the District Manager of the German Labor Front; indeed, he doesn't like the German Labor Front at all. Karl is the managing director of a timber-processing firm in lower Mühlviertel and refuses to buy a Labor Front flag from the District Manager. Nor does he want to give a company donation to the front. And on top of all that, Karl Gumpelmaier even sends the poor District Manager a warning, just because the latter hasn't paid for the firewood that he ordered for his own private use. To even things out, District Manager Gerstl sends a group of people to Karl Gumpelmaier who take him away because about that time the Labor Front official had received a useful notification which empowers him, and indeed all the mayors in the region, as well as the NSDAP District Leaders, the Sub-prefects, the Employment Exchanges, and many more besides, to get rid of the likes of the tiresome Karl with no consequences.

Right at the former border with the Old Reich in the extreme southwest of the Innviertel, in a little town by the name of St. Pantaleon, resourceful minds have just set about establishing an immensely practical Labor Education Camp, which is shortly to be accepting fellow citizens *who refuse on principle to work, who constantly sneak off, incessantly stir up trouble in the workplace, or refuse to accept any offer of work, although they are physically able to perform it. But they must all have reached the age of 18. Asocial managing directors are also included. Only cases of a criminal nature are beyond the reach of this body*, as are the severely wounded, because *heavy physical work has to be done. Out-and-out habitual beggars are unwelcome because they are not motivated to work.*

Oskar Heinrich and Heinrich Müller are indeed, without a doubt, *Volksgenossen*, yet they're far from being eighteen years of age. In practice, however, that doesn't matter at all. The lads make the assiduous Steyermühl Papermill Company Youth Counsellor white with rage, because they're entirely unwilling to train and play soccer with his Hitler Youth squad, not today and not ever. The two youths are summarily dismissed, although, surprisingly, they are reinstated again after sixteen days. They now indeed appear to be reformed and even prepared to shoot and defend against goals. During the first match, however, one of them promptly gets into a heated exchange of blows with the above-mentioned Youth Counsellor, who has just heard about the notification. And what a piece of luck! The camp accepts the two of them.

Vladimir Bezdek is indeed, without a doubt, already of age, yet he's not a *Volksgenosse*. In practice, however, that doesn't matter at all. The thirty-one-year-old mechanic from Clouboky near Brunn has been working diligently for years in the regional capital of Linz and has recently started dating a German girl. Word soon gets around in the firm, and one of the community of mechanics goes, duty bound, to the boss and reports the flagrant violation of popular sentiment. The boss has just filed the notification containing the practical decree issued by the Gauleiter and simply tries his luck. For Vladimir, the camp gates are wide open.

In the hamlet of Weyer, district of St. Pantaleon, there's an impressive farmstead with affiliated pub, extensive stabling, and what was once over one hundred acres of land. It belongs to Germans from Bavaria, who acquired the property shortly after the First World War. In the whole area, the Geratsdorfers were the only ones who saw no grounds at the time of the Austrian Corporate State to join the Patriotic Front. At the Starhemberg assemblies, the decision was therefore taken on the spot to boycott their pub. In the end, the farm owners even had to start to sell land to pay off beer debts.

Even now, after the *Anschluss* and the start of the war, there's usually more room in the pub lounge than the landlord likes. Most of the natives still remain extremely wary about many things associated with the new order. To make matters worse, the farmer fell off the roof two years ago, and since then his right leg has only been of limited use. The farmer's wife had an operation, which cost them one of their cows, and they foolishly and without thinking acted as guarantors for a lot of money to a certain Mr. Gluck, and that turned out to be even more expensive. Naturally, Mayor Michael Kaltenberger knows about the financial problems of the family with its three children. He therefore has in mind to pitch his longed-for Education Camp on their property; that would be the ideal spot.

This Mr. Kaltenberger not only holds the office of

mayor, but also, as we've already learned, heads the St. Pantaleon Local Unit of the NSDAP and functions as chairman of the Water Cooperative. He is the registrar, runs the village pub, and, in addition also has his own farm, which stretches over a good thirty hectares. Beyond that he's a well-known cattle dealer for miles around. As one colleague to another, in the spirit of friendship, he makes the following tempting offer to landlord and farmer Max Geratsdorfer, who is in such dire straits that he is unable to reject it: I'll lease the house and farm for six years, including all the cattle, grazing and arable land, and will make a decent investment in the buildings because the Party wants to set up an exemplary Education Camp here. If the camp closes before that time's up, which is highly unlikely, the lease agreement will be declared null and void after a few months' notice. At any rate, by that time your children will be grown up and can take over.

In Kaltenberger's centrally located pub there's always a lot going on. Just recently masses of women gathered in their Sunday best for the impressive Mother's Day celebrations. The highlight was of course the official honoring of German mothers with the award of the Mother's Cross in Gold, Silver, and Bronze. Of course, the honorable District Party Group Leader, whose wife Theresia stands loyally at his side as leader of the District Women's League, doesn't miss the opportunity to be the one to put the deserved award round the neck of all sixty-seven qualifying district inhabitants and makes extensive references to their important role in securing the fate of the German nation.

By pure chance we arrive exactly when there are veritable hordes of people queuing outside the multipurpose hall, which also serves as a movie theater. Twice in a row the screening of the box-office success *Dawn* is completely sold out. The unmistakable message of the extravagant submarine spectacular, set during the First

World War, is that under Nationalist Socialist leadership it is impossible for a Germany which produces heroes like these to lose a war. By way of proof, the latest weekly newsreel garnishes the film's propaganda message with spiced-up documentary material about the brilliant campaign triumph in the west. The old arch-enemy France has just capitulated, and England will be next in line to have to admit defeat.

It's therefore really no surprise that Michael Kaltenberger was recently cut to the quick by a provocative guest: the man refused to agree with the landlord's verdict that the war would be over by the coming autumn. In the evening news at ten, it had just been reported that Calais had fallen, and the landlord gave England a few more weeks at most, *to which I retorted that this war would last as long as the World War, or indeed even longer, and that both America and Russia would also become involved. Then Kaltenberger came over to me, accused me of being a bad German, and hit me twice in the face, which cost me two teeth.* This incident will, of course, have repercussions. Very soon the outspoken pub guest will receive a summons from the Gestapo.

The mood among most of the farming families in the locality, however, remains cautious to antagonistic, despite the flood of propaganda. The Party therefore sees itself obliged to perform visible good deeds at a local level, to reinforce the promise of the grand vision. Suitable premises are just being prepared on which to set up a so-called Harvest-Kindergarten, so this year farmers and farmhands will be able to concentrate exclusively on harvesting grain and vegetables without worrying about the younger generation. Meat has been rationed for a long time now, and it wouldn't be easy to cope with a failed harvest.

The Education Camp's freshly recruited and very impressive squad of guards consists exclusively of little Führers.

8

In civilian life, these gentlemen hadn't hitherto risen beyond the lower rungs of the ladder to success, whereas in their dashing brown uniforms they've long since risen above the civilian rank and file and are entitled to call themselves Senior Staff Sergeant, Troop Leader, Senior Troop Leader, and Storm Leader of SA [Storm Troopers] Regiment 159. That sounds exceptionally good. At long last, they're being given serious responsibilities, and it does indeed make them a little proud to hold positions that in similar institutions are reserved for the elite SS.

Fresh walls and barbed wire secure the site; a vehicle is just coming through the gate. Karl Gumpelmaier has to get out; the journey has taken several hours. But it is also possible that Karl, like many people who share the same fate, will arrive by train, since motor vehicles may in fact still only be used to a limited extent, even by Party officials. The railway employees soon have an eye for little groups like this one of male travelers whose destination is Bürmoos, the nearest station, from which not all of them will set off a few hours later on the return journey, visibly relaxed. Even if we can't say exactly how Karl Gumpelmaier is brought here, we don't need to speculate about what happens to him afterwards; we know that.

The fellows were not exactly talkative when they took him away. They didn't tell him why they were picking him up, or where the journey was going. He's more than just a little bit angry. He'll tell those men what's what, that's for sure. On the way to the camp administration office, he sees out of the corner of his eye some people who don't look well at all. Karl Gumpelmaier is briefly irritated. Once inside with the Camp Director, he tries to bang on the table, talks about arbitrariness, protests vehemently about the ludicrous reasons for bringing him here, reasons which are now being briefly read aloud to him, but the first carefully aimed butcher's punch is already hitting him; the blood is warm on his face. Gumpelmaier will have to change his habits right away.

Outside the camp, everyday life goes on relatively quietly. In 1940 the war is a long way off, and in this early summer the grain is already high; it's primarily farmers who live here. Most of the inhabitants of Haigermoos and the surrounding area were relatively pleased with the newly reorganized Austrian State, the clergy and lay authorities clad in traditional costume. On the other hand, many people find the Nazis offensive. Stolid farmers complain, in asides, that they're stupid lads who've learned nothing and are no good at anything, that they're strutting around like cockerels, in all sorts of uniforms, acting like lords and spending the whole God-given day doing nothing. They crack bawdy jokes about the honorable priest and the divine order, and aren't only crude when they've had too much to drink.

The few houses in Weyer also belong to tiny Haigermoos with its seven or more square kilometers of land. After the *Anschluss*, nobody was prepared to act as the Nazi mayor; that is, they did install one, but he got himself a medical note authorizing dismissal after a few weeks. It seemed he had nerve trouble. So the village was summarily incorporated into the district. In the larger neighboring community of St. Pantaleon, there is in fact no shortage of swastika-wearers. There's nothing that can be done about it, except pray and wait and see. And don't look when early every morning the SA herds the tottering prisoners through forest and field, a good three kilometers to the little river in Waidmoos.

The curlew still breeds there regularly, and it will be thirty-six years until the hunting club complains about the final disappearance of the black grouse. A few kilometers further to the southeast, peat has been cut on an industrial scale since the eighties, and now the whole remaining marshy area is to be collared. As early as 1935, the draining of the Ibmer Moor was once tackled, but the ambitious project was soon terminated for lack of money. Now the National Socialists are taking a new run at it and in all want to drain no less than three thousand seven hundred hectares. As many as fifty-two farms are to be set up within this area; it's a gigantic undertaking. The Moosach, the little river whose bed they want to redirect for this purpose, forms the natural boundary with Salzburg.

By no means all the able-bodied men have gone to war yet; many have found jobs, and their daily bread at the Water Authority. So as of now hefty smallholders and farm laborers from the surrounding district, together with the inmates of the camp, are moving enormous loads of soil and are lining the new riverbanks with granite rocks. In order that everything be clear, right after the first non-voluntary colleagues are brought in, the civilian workers are informed by Government Head of Planning, Dipl. Engineer Langgartner, Mayor Kaltenberger, and Camp Director Staudinger, on the occasion of a work-site roll call, that it may well happen that the detainees will be punished and beaten while on the job. Strict silence is to be observed in this matter, and those disobeying will face severe repercussions; indeed, they could, with luck, be allowed to continue working on the building site but only as prisoners.

Johann Gabauer has drunk a lot in the course of his life. Also worked a lot, but that's a long time ago now. For the idyllic, climatically favored village on the southern edge of the Bohemian Forest in which many years ago this native of Vienna ended up, Hans is to this very day merely a shadowy newcomer. For some time, alcohol has been doing substantial damage to Gabauer's body; the slightly built man is sickly; he's now fifty-three, looks seventy, neglects himself, but doesn't go so far as to die. It would be lying to claim that anyone still enjoyed his company. So it's a relief that the new powers-that-be recently declared themselves prepared to take on even apparently hopeless cases like this habitual drinker and turn them into decent human beings. So off to the camp with him.

Ferdinand Hammerschmied will not meet him because, when he arrives, Johann Gabauer has already been murdered. For Hammerschmied, a carpenter by trade and an active National Socialist, it is extremely painful that he suddenly finds himself in this wretched, corrective institution among all the antisocial elements. It's all because of his loose tongue. If he'd held back from taking part in the noisy altercation and not reminded his turncoat boss in front of witnesses of his earlier membership in the Communist Republican Defense Alliance, he might have been spared a number of things. Even so, in his case, Camp Commandant Staudinger waives the customary welcome thrashing. Compassionate Party Comrades at home in Nettingsdorf immediately set all the wheels in motion, and four weeks later, Ferdinand is released the day before Christmas Eve, 1940. He has to certify in writing that he has heard and seen nothing.

Few people can believe what they hear and see during these months, thrown together from all walks of life, slogging away here, until many collapse and others die. Johann Gabauer is the first. The SA Guard Troop quickly finds out that he's the very weakest of them all, that being deprived of alcohol causes him severe problems, that it's fun to humiliate him. He remains so nice and humble. In the middle of July, Johann collapses on the building site for no visible reason. When he wakes up from his coma, they beat him so severely with rubber truncheons on his naked torso that he has to be taken back to the camp in a wheelbarrow. Every day when his powers fail and he's too weak to go on working, the same game is repeated; thrashing, kicks, mock drowning in the river. Finally, the end of his saga of suffering is foreseeable: today none other than the Camp Administrator in person thrashes him, then draws out his official dagger and threatens to stab him to death. Shortly thereafter, another guard asks the delinquent to give a definitive response as to whether he should be shot or drowned. Gabauer meekly asks Troop Leader Josef Mayrlehner that he be allowed to drown himself. He is granted this privilege. Johann totters out into the deeper water. Suddenly he cries out loud for help and gesticulates wildly so that it looks from some distance away as if he's splashing around happily. Fellow prisoners have to pull the pitiful figure out of the water; once again he's beaten till he loses consciousness. He doesn't wake up again so quickly. Gabauer lies in his wet things on a cart for hours on this cool, windy summer's day and is finally transported off to the district doctor.

The doctor is also the camp physician. In the village, people aren't too keen on the fact that whenever he is needed out there with the criminals he simply abandons his long-time patients to cope without him. And they often need him in the camp. He's usually out there three or four times a week, and there are emergency cases in addition. He inspects everything, treats wounds, hypothermia, even takes people with fairly serious injuries in his own car to the hospital, but still does nothing to stop the assaults. There are camp regulations according to which the physical punishment of the inmates is prohibited on principle; the rules don't mention murder. For three days, Dr. Straffner treats the dying Johann Gabauer in the camp; he writes pneumonia on the death certificate. The corpse ends up without much ado in the parish cemetery where there's still sufficient room, as the prisoners learn from their smirking guards. Nobody anywhere else misses Johann.

St. Pantaleon's priest can't give the man with the same first name a Christian burial, even if he wants to; he's been held in detention awaiting trial for several weeks in the Linz Gestapo prison. His list of sins is long: precisely at the times when everybody knows the Hitler Youth groups are holding roll calls in the village, he blithely offers so-called Christian teaching for young people in his church and simply ignores the rules of the District Air Defense Headquarters with reference to the ringing of church bells. An attempted collection for the benefit of the Capuchin monks is also on the list of his offenses. *On May 10, 1940, he paid an evening visit in his parish village to the home of one Johanna Nussbaumer, the wife of a hauler and not a member of his circle of followers, in order to collect a parcel.* The two get to talking about this and that, including possible dangers threatening German soldiers in Norway.

On the way to Mrs. Nussbaumer, the Reverend Father bumps into the mayor. Later when the Gestapo question the priest in the district offices, Hitler Youths report what they overheard while eavesdropping in front of the open window and immediately conveyed to District Party Group Leader Kaltenberger: Johann Fuchs, sixty-two years old, unmarried, priest in St. Pantaleon, doesn't wish to believe either what the enemy radio stations report or what ours say. Furthermore, he explains ironically to the dismayed Mrs. Nussbaumer, an expelled follower of other circles, verbatim: *Even in World War I, it was always said that the Germans would win, win, win, and finally they did indeed win, until they were crushed.* In a letter to his aged mother from prison, intercepted as a precaution, which backs up the charge most impressively, the accused clergyman actually goes so far as to make the impertinent assertion that times are such that it is not the worst people who are now sitting in jail.

Sebastian Riess is an agricultural worker and doesn't get along with his employer's maid. I'm leaving, he says on

14

the eleventh of August, 1940, to the farmer's wife, and sets off on foot with a small suitcase full of laundry to the area of Pinzgau, in the Salzburg region, where he grew up. At the entrance to the village of St. Pantaleon, he stops at a farm for a brief rest. A short time later, three gentlemen appear, who are introduced to Sebastian as Mayor Michael Kaltenberger, Camp Commandant August Staudinger, and guard Josef Mayrlehner. A lively discussion ensues about this and that. The farm laborer in transit thinks Franz Kubinger's good idea isn't a good idea at all. In his view, Sebastian says at some point in the conversation, this region, incidentally, is still Austria and not the Third Reich.

At this point, August Staudinger doesn't wish to continue the discussion. He turns serious. A hefty blow of the fist bounces Sebastian against the wooden garden fence. His lower lip immediately swells up and he's taken off to the camp. *After he's admitted, screams are heard from the Education Camp and soon afterwards it appeared that Riess was a good deal more seriously injured than when he was admitted. He had blue and green areas of discoloring on his head.* These stem from ten blows of a rubber truncheon to the left side of the head, always on the same spot, inflicted during the first night by the boss in person, who doesn't shirk from overtime when it comes to educating people. He thus actually succeeds within just a few hours in convincing the newcomer that his knowledge of geography is, regrettably, not up to date. In the following weeks, Sebastian Riess will always be given priority as a candidate for beating until he won't stop spitting blood. Dr. Straffner will finally have him taken to a hospital as a precaution.

From the neighboring village of Roding up on a nearby hill on the other side of the Salzburg county border on a clear day, there is a wonderful panoramic view of the Alps to the south, across the undulating, sparsely populated, hilly landscape, right on to the northern horizon. Even on cloudy days, the river below can be seen. During these months, there's a lot going on there; nothing stays hidden from the population. Furthermore, some Water Board workers don't keep their mouths as tightly shut as they were instructed. The inhabitants grumble more and more, get worked up, mostly about the fact that the SA, apparently as a special form of humiliation, utter wild threats to urge Czech prisoners to carry out beatings of German, that is Austrian, fellow sufferers, and to make them as juicy as possible, so the blood spurts out.

But let's also have a little look down there: prisoners in groups of three are pushing wheelbarrows of earth, with a capacity of three-quarters of a cubic meter, on temporary tracks, initially on the flat, then more steeply uphill. Twenty-five journeys per shift, plus loading, are the absolute minimum. With their poor footwear, often only crude wooden clogs, it's exhausting work for the poor workers, particularly when it's raining and wet. Time and time again they slip and fall to the ground, the wheelbarrow threatens to slide back, and they try with all their might to stop it. A guard, who wishes to be called an educator, stands at the steepest point. With his rubber truncheon, he searches out the weakest of the trio, and drums on his back till the remaining two somehow or other manage on their own to reach the top. If the vehicle goes out of their control or even overturns on the return journey, they too can brace themselves for a beating. It has once again just got to that point, and a civilian worker operating in the vicinity screams angrily at Alois Rosenbichler: If we lose the war, they'll tear you apart! But the latter only gives his victim a brief moment's respite, grins broadly, and says: We won't lose the war.

As an undernourished, forced-labor victim, one should, if at all possible, get by at the building site without a circulatory collapse. Otherwise one will swiftly be knocked back into consciousness. One should also, as one barely eighteen-year-old youth did, not get one's left foot stuck in the tracks of the freight railway. *Because of this delay in carrying out the work, Alois Rosenbichler dealt him such hefty blows to the head with the rubber club that Schmidhuber fell over. While he was lying on the ground with his foot still stuck there, Rosenbichler kicked him in the face with the toe of his boot so that Schmidhuber was slightly injured on the lips and the area around his left eye. Furthermore, in order to force him to get up during the maltreatment with the rubber club, Rosenbichler threatened to shoot him dead. But because Schmidhuber couldn't get up and became unconscious as a consequence of the maltreatment, he had to be carried into the camp by fellow prisoners.*

Franz Ennsthaler from Sierning, fifty years of age, is so beaten up on the building site at the end of August 1940 that he's only fit for the cemetery, but he wakes up again briefly in hospital. Between beatings, he was thrown repeatedly into the water and held under, he whispers into the ear of the doctor in charge. They leave the three-quarters-dead man propped soaking wet against a bench for hours, a fundamental part of the educational measures, as is well known, and meanwhile all around people slog away industriously. The medic sees to the autopsy. Results: bloodstained, superficial epithelial defects extending over the whole back, especially on the prominent parts of the back, as well as on the back of the head and upper arm. Cause of death: cerebral bleeding. Again, doctors see everything and do nothing.

Slightly late, and without mention of petty details like murder and beating to death, the interested general public learns in mid-September on how Franz Kubinger's good idea has become raw reality. The newspaper can report many edifying tales: *On the instructions of the Gauleiter, a Labor Education Camp for work-shy elements was established in St.*

Pantaleon. Despite its short existence, the camp has already clearly proven itself to be a beneficial establishment. The detainees are in fact being assigned to the drainage work in Ibm-Waidmoos, and, with the help of this additional work force, the urgent project to drain the Ibm-Waidmoos area is moving towards a more rapid completion.

At seventeen, the now twenty-three-year-old SA Senior Staff Sergeant Alois Rosenbichler migrated from nearby Ostermiething to the acclaimed German Reich, where he made his living as a painter's assistant. After the upheaval, he returned briefly to his native country and finally was among the soldiers who conquered Poland. Later discharged from the German Army as unfit for duty because of a stomach complaint, he turned down the civilian post offered to him by the welfare officer and followed instead the call of his regiment leader to join the Guard Unit in Weyer. Against extremely tough competition, he very soon earned the reputation among the prisoners of being the most brutal, the most sadistic of all the guards.

For Alois Rosenbichler himself, his excesses of violence did not, however, cause him any sleeplessness at all. Countless witnesses will later confirm to the Senior Public Prosecutor that Rosenbichler often slept like a lamb in the sentry hut on the building site. *If he woke up, he would fall on the nearest available camp inmate for no reason and brutalize him indiscriminately with a rubber truncheon. His blows were so powerful that the inmates collapsed and remained lying there unconscious. He repeatedly punched them and with his hobnailed hiking boots, dealt kicks to the head and other sensitive body areas of the prisoners lying on the ground. Another time he hit out in a blind rage at the detainees because they wanted to buy a loaf from someone who had appeared on the building site carrying bread.*

Seventy-five pfennigs a day is what, according to the camp regulations, the prisoners may spend on their own personal needs, if the guards allow it. Bread and cigarettes are the most sought-after goods. Despite permission in principle, buying them may be risky and even spell death if the SA are in a bad mood. Smoking during work is, without exception, strictly prohibited. Anyone who nevertheless risks it and is caught has to pay with a severe beating. Prisoners who try to write to their relatives saying they are suffering bitterly from hunger and begging them for a food parcel are dealt with by the Camp Director, who, after careful reading of relevant sections of the letters, beats them up for days for attempting to spread infamous lies.

Late that summer in the village of Laubenbach, a few hundred meters up river, an unusually high number of apples are peeled and then cooked into apple sauce. As it's practically impossible to pass anything to the starving inmates, sympathetic souls throw the peelings piece by piece into the water. The current carries along the unobtrusive little ships to the prisoners, who gobble them up greedily if there are no guards in the vicinity. At least, this is the anecdote which will still be told decades later, and we would like to think that it was not merely a figment of someone's imagination.

The SA like taking along the Alsatians. Two of these dogs, a young one and a fully grown one, belong to Chief Troop Leader Josef Wieger. As soon as the men who've been beaten cower helplessly on the ground, the older dog, which has been trained to be aggressive, is set on the half-conscious men and allowed to bite their arms and legs. Such a thing is evidently entertaining for the guard staff, but the mood in nearby Roding, which belongs to St. Georgen on the Salzach, continues to worsen because of such sights, especially when one day a civilian worker's thigh is inadvertently bitten. Even the farmer on whose ground the building site lies ends up being attacked by the SA dog, when he's merely surveying the situation. The mayor of St. Georgen finally sees himself obliged to use the official notice board to take his own population to task, rather than reprimand the Camp Commandant. Without further ado, he threatens with the Gestapo all those who can't keep their mouths shut and who have the cheek to pass comments on the conditions down there by the river.

Anton Leidenfrost can usually trust his nose. He opens the window and soaks in the warm, damp air; no doubt about it, today is mushroom weather. He's already grabbing his basket and heading off cheerfully into the nearby wood. The unexpectedly meager harvest soon disappoints him, and he decides to try his luck further off. But further over there is too far in his direction for guard Josef Wieger. He spies the intruder a few hundred meters away from the building site on the edge of the wood, makes his way as noiselessly as he can towards him, and aims the muzzle of his service pistol directly at the chest of the man who is completely taken aback: Get out of here, or I'll shoot you to pieces! are the alternatives he offers. Mr. Leidenfrost, who as Party Member and police officer is himself extremely well versed in the keeping of National Socialist law and order, has for the moment lost all desire for mushrooms.

Josef Wieger, the trained shoemaker, is now forty-three, and he's been a National Socialist since the late twenties. Before his promotion to Camp Educator, he was working as a civilian workshop manager in Infantry Regiment 135 in Simbach and also two days a week as a cinema operator on the other bank of the river Inn in Braunau. Wieger may indeed in principle not have the slightest doubt that he's dealing with completely degenerate, depraved subjects, who only respond to brutality. Yet sometimes this man, alone of all the guards, is overcome by changes of mood that don't tally at all with what's otherwise reported about him. Now and again, it actually comes to pass that he secretly slips prisoners a cigarette, and on days when the frost hangs on the whole day long, his wife appeared on one occasion with a huge container full of hot tea for the slave laborers who are blue with the cold.

Alois Kreil is eighteen and has just successfully completed his apprenticeship. Now he'd like to find a new employer as quickly as possible. The owner of the firm, a respected manufacturer of farm machines, does not in fact want the lad to take his journeyman's exam. Alois protests, his boss goes hotfoot to the Braunau town council to complain, and says he wants them to free him of this asocial young man, who only has to work three Sundays in succession for him and doesn't want to devote the fourth to the Hitler Youth. This request naturally meets with a favorable response.

Ferdinand Hochmayr has to pay thirty Reichsmarks maintenance per month and is twelve weeks in arrears when he's admitted to the camp on this account. By way of welcome, August Staudinger knocks out all the incisors and molars of his upper jaw. Anton Denk, on the other hand, has left his workplace without permission for four days to help a farmer with the harvest. Denk can't feed his large family adequately from his wages in the Ranshofen aluminum works, probably also because he's not averse to having a few drinks too many. The farmer promised him food in return for good hard work. When he's admitted, the guard finds two cigarettes in the delinquent's waistcoat. On this particular day that's manifestly undesirable. Guard August Winkler, who's soon thereafter to take premature leave of the team of educators, therefore immediately strikes the surprised Anton to the ground himself, before he pushes him off to Staudinger's office for further treatment. The latter acts as usual. After twenty blows to the face, the new man is bleeding from mouth and nose and lying unconscious on the ground. *I am the father of twelve children, of farming stock, was in the military for three years, and four years fighting on the Front in World War I, possess the Silver Medal for Bravery Class II and the Bronze Bravery Medal, and had to put up with this treatment by Staudinger.*

The verdict of the Special Court in Linz is that the priest Johann Fuchs has, without a shadow of a doubt, acted against the law. Six months in prison is a relatively mild sentence. Yet the clergyman is hardly free before he's arrested again. After being reported for stealing electric current and then spending several months in detention awaiting trial, the trial ends this time in an embarrassing acquittal. In order to avoid such slip-ups in future, his next misdeed is maliciously publicized in the newspaper with the friendly support of influential circles. We will obtain a copy in good time and may now already expect a dog and an anonymous lady as incorruptible witnesses. In the end, the Reverend Fuchs is forbidden to set foot in St. Pantaleon. His successor, Kajetan Laux, a substitute priest and Capuchin monk, will quickly have to learn that alert ears feel duty bound to report provocative sermons to the local Party leadership. His trial will take place in Berlin. Undermining the military's defense capability is an accusation that can cost you your life.

Not that anyone seriously believes that the National Socialist Motor Transport Corps is unknown in this rural idyll. Even if the dream of the affordable people's car, the Volkswagen for the masses, has proven premature because of the constraints of war, many are united in their fascination with their own vehicles. Soon there's even a gas station opened within the town boundaries, and obstacles to delivery are bridged, but then the supply itself collapses. The future operator of this gas station, who's also technical advisor to the Wildshut Assault Unit of the NSMTC, truly can't complain about insufficient public interest in his training evenings in the brewery pub. This time Karl Hiebler has chosen the broad topic "Secrets of the Engine" – somehow sounds exciting.

Certainly, somewhere among the listeners there sits NSMTC Troop Leader Hans Mells. A large Salzburg brewery bought and closed a small competitor in Wildshut. Party Member Mells administers the firm's estate, by now substantially enlarged to include a slaughterhouse and the brewery pub in which Karl Hiebler is using his pointer to explain a cross-section of a water-cooled four-cylinder engine. The local Party also has Hans Mells as its organizational head and member of the Town Council. This reminds us that up to now we've completely neglected to pay a visit to the local council appointed by Mayor Michael Kaltenberger.

It meets somewhat irregularly under Kaltenberger's superb chairmanship. The sessions mostly turn out gratifyingly short; decisions are made unanimously on principle, no trace is left of the former gossip-shop atmosphere. Here's a small selection of agenda items dealt with: St. Pantaleon makes a noteworthy contribution of four thousand Reichsmarks to the draining of Ibm-Waidmoos; as quickly as possible, a suitable piece of land is to be purchased for the establishment of the district sports grounds; Hermann Kronberger is to be taken immediately to the institution in Hartheim; the basic tax rate for the financial year 1941 is fixed at a hundred per cent, the new drink tax at ten per cent; for the purpose of awarding the Mother's Cross, all mothers with four and more children are to be registered; the community land is to be divided into nine districts for the purpose of counting livestock; Fritz Greilbauer is transferred without further explanation for three months to Dachau concentration camp, and the raising of a bridging loan of five thousand Reichsmarks from the People's Bank in Oberndorf is approved. In order to signal their assent, Karl Hiebler, Hans Mells, and Dr. Alois Straffner, all of whom in the meantime are well known to us, regularly raise their arms and later duly sign the minutes of the session.

We permit ourselves to give a brief outline of the consequences of two of these decisions. Eleven months have elapsed since the removal of the forty-three-year-old Fritz to Dachau, when the community of St. Pantaleon gets a small parcel and the official news that Mr. Friedrich Greilbauer, mechanic, fell victim in 1940 to a heart attack in Mauthausen concentration camp. In order to be able to settle the estate in accordance with regulations, a list of the attached effects is appended for clarification: *1 hat, 2 pairs of trousers, 1 shirt, 1 pair of shoes, 2 jackets, 1 pullover, 1 pair of socks.* Hermann Kronberger, for his part, after eleven years spent with his family, soon must be classified as unworthy of life, and will, together with approximately twenty thousand other people entitled to euthanasia, simply have his life concluded peacefully and quietly in Hartheim Castle, a lunatic asylum not far from Linz. *Disinfection* is the jargon term for this procedure. For the record, we note that the District Council in St. Pantaleon initially of course could not foresee in detail the impact of their decisions at a wider level and in the longer term. But they see daily with their own eyes what's going on in and around the redesigning of the river Moosach. It's not less barbaric, and in the end there's often enough a cynically fabricated cause of death given here as well.

Today, for once, there's to be a change in the otherwise monotonous camp routine. The prisoners are herded directly from work to a community reception in the mayor's village pub. Führer Adolf Hitler has extraordinarily important things to communicate via the ether waves to his hard-working munitions workers, things which can't in any circumstances even be kept from asocial elements. On the way back to the building site via the Kugelberg hill, the fifty-one-year-old Anton Atzelsberger, nicknamed "Caretaker," a particular favorite with the education staff, suddenly collapses. The severely exhausted man receives at least forty blows for that, until even the raging Alois Rosenbichler himself has no strength left. A few more hefty kicks to the head, then another SA man is supposed to carry on. The latter lays into the victim for a while longer, finally draws his pistol, and says he'll shoot him now if he doesn't get up immediately. Atzelsberger doesn't react. The next kick to the head makes Anton's tongue stick out of his mouth; the tortured man is in his death throes. Now SA Chief Troop Leader Josef Wieger stands with both feet on the lump of flesh under him. Blood pours from the anus and drenches the trousers. Two Czech fellow prisoners have to drag the lifeless body back into the camp. The SA officer invites the two men to carry on diligently ill-treating the malingerer.

The next day the Camp Administration summons the district doctor. The latter establishes that the patient has lost an extremely large amount of blood. *In the bed in which he had spent the night there was a large pool of tar-colored runny stools which seeped through the straw sack and had led to a further pool on the floor.* Dr. Straffner has the dying remains of Anton Atzelsberger taken immediately to Salzburg hospital, where he is still alive when admitted. *Status praesens: Diminished state of nutrition, extreme paleness of the skin and the visible mucous membranes, deteriorating physical condition.* A few hours later, it's all over. Official cause of death: burst stomach ulcer.

The washerwoman employed in the camp isn't pleased by such occurrences. Every day, traces of the blood-stained shirts and the soiled underwear are left to the hardworking woman. Yet she doesn't dare to demand higher pay. In that respect, the Regional General Medical Insurance Company in Linz is significantly stricter. It receives so many such notices of illness-related absences in this Labor Education Camp officially run by the District Welfare Organization that it sees itself compelled to intervene immediately for financial reasons. Medical experts are to scrutinize the state of affairs in the camp. The Medical Insurance Company's official doctor thus sets off on his way to Weyer but quickly seems satisfied with the explanation that the susceptibility of the inmates is to be put down to their earlier dubious lifestyle. Nobody is examined; rather, the Camp Administration soon thereafter receives the information that the premium for the above-mentioned group of insured parties must be substantially increased right away. Commandant August Staudinger takes the news calmly. The prisoners have to pay for the privilege themselves anyway, namely out of their wages, once the education costs have been deducted. The inmates' wages are deposited in a blocked account, so that in the event that they emerge alive from the camp, Storm Leader Gottfried Haimbuchner, in charge of administration by virtue of his rank, can, if so inclined, actually open the coffers on their departure.

At this point, Party Member Government Head of Planning Ewald Langgartner, Dip. Eng., from the Water Authority offices in Braunau, explains to us in brief the organizational details of the work deployment of education prisoners within the framework of the Ibm-Waidmoos Drainage Project. *By request of the Camp Management, or rather the government official in charge of it, Party Comrade Kubinger, the inmates of the camp have to work sixty hours per week without payment for overtime. There is therefore no question of a payment for overtime by the Construction Management because the Construction Management is not interested in people doing overtime.* We may thus assume that the authorities fight tooth and nail against the work mania of the prisoners but heroically succumb and finally don't stop them. Instead of a fixed-rate lodging charge, the honorable Dip. Engineer continues, those compulsorily employed men would receive board and lodging gratis. The wages would be seen to by Camp Director August Staudinger or his Deputy Administrator Gottfried Haimbuchner, and the Construction Management would not be able to exert any influence on how they were used.

Ferdinand Duböck is fifty-seven. He has a long, snow-white beard. The prematurely aged man hasn't been able to manage properly for weeks now, and the strain has simply been too much for him. Yesterday evening, he had just laboriously cut up his food into small pieces, when SA Troop Leader Josef Mayrlehner ordered him to shove his plate over to another camp inmate. While the fellow sufferer greedily wolfed down the extra ration, Ferdinand had to stand at attention beside the table. And now the guard forced him to say "Thanks very much" when the plate was empty. Ferdinand gasped out the words "Thanks very much." Then he was allowed to take part in the singing lesson on an empty stomach.

Today he's feeling particularly ill, is shaking, and isn't keeping down any of his meager breakfast. As punishment he gets a one-pound loaf of bread hurled by the guard with full force in his face from less than a meter away, which knocks Ferdinand off the bench. This unseemly behavior positively screams out for further education measures. The rubber truncheon serves to put the defenseless man in the mood for the working day ahead.

Josef Mayrlehner, previously a carpenter's assistant, has in recent times got himself a fine whip made of leather straps and now uses it on the building site to tear Ferdinand Duböck's face to pieces. This goes on for a quarter of an hour. Ferdinand has had enough and mumbles that he wants to hang himself. Josef Mayrlehner considers that a viable proposition. He fetches a rope, gives it to the man whose beard is by now speckled with blood, and proposes the tool shed as the scene of the suicide. Duböck enters and tries to hang himself. But the frayed rope breaks. Ferdinand, already unconscious, with strangulation furrows round his neck, lies blue in his own blood. When he opens his eyes some time later, the rubber truncheons flail down on him. Later in the camp, Josef Mayrlehner wishes, for the sake of regularity, that the man who has failed would finally have another go at his promised suicide. Josef kindly offers to procure a second rope as a favor and this time raises the question of banisters. Fellow-prisoners who want to intervene are chased away; others stand alongside and watch aghast. Shaking and with painful slowness, Ferdinand Duböck makes fast the rope, knots the noose, puts it around his neck, climbs up to the banisters and drops. This rope also splits; to complicate matters, the unlucky chap splits open his forehead, lies unconscious on the hall floor, and is still not completely dead.

For months now, asocial male creatures, already more than one hundred and thirty of them in total, have been streaming here from the whole Reich province of Oberdonau, settling into this idyllically situated camp in order to enjoy a proper education at long last. *The country, whose nature, culture, and people represent a unity that could only be destroyed by political powers hostile to the Reich, thus seems to be a veritable cradle of united thinking, feeling, and behaving. We flatter ourselves that these virtues may have helped build the Führer's greatness.* Party Comrade Certified Engineer Ewald Langgartner, the deserving Construction Manager of the ambitious Drainage Project, can look up these edifying lines in the comfort of his own home, since he's recently just been honored at a dignified ceremony by the award of a prestigious book (from which we're taking these fundamental thoughts) from District Party Group Leader Kaltenberger for his exemplary contribution as NSDAP Training Leader.

The third edition of the sumptuous coffee-table book *Oberdonau, the Homeland of the Führer* is just being rushed into print because of the great demand, when integrated thinking, feeling, and behaving is being drummed into the hitherto embarrassingly work-shy camp inmates, using all available means, such as, for example, tearing off prisoner Franz Kaspar's left ear. The local population, daily involuntary witnesses to what the Senior Public Prosecutor will describe in strong terms as atrocities and monstrosities, hears meanwhile over the brand-new and affordable People's Radio 301 Wn, along with propaganda speeches and jubilant announcements of battle victories, the hits of this autumn 1940, such as Peter Kreuder's *In Life Everything Comes to an End* or excerpts from Nico Dostal's operetta *Flight into Happiness*.

Many prisoners also attempt flight. Yet as a rule, that turns out extremely badly for them. "Caretaker" Anton Atzelsberger could tell a tale or two about that, were he still alive. By an early attempt to escape he made himself quite unpopular. A bullet stops him after just a few meters. For five weeks, he lies in hospital with severe gunshot wounds, then returns to camp. He knows exactly what's in store for him there: they make an example of Atzelsberger to deter the others; they do it slowly, but thoroughly. We've already reported it.

In his capacity as mayor, Michael Kaltenberger has the special pleasure, with widespread popular support, of opening a new small-caliber shooting range for the district. The hard-working members of the St. Pantaleon Fire

Prevention Society, founded in 1932 by district physician Dr. Alois Straffner, have invested countless voluntary hours of work, and now two modern ranges, one a hundred and ten meters, the other fifty meters long, are available for all to use. This is announced in the popular weekly paper *New Watch on the Inn*.

The SA is extremely well integrated into village life. District Council Karl Hiebler, for instance, is particularly fond of chatting with August Staudinger about St. Pantaleon inhabitants who have disappeared for political reasons. The guard team is, after all, extremely well informed about everything. The guards for their part are happy, in an appropriate context, to supply the Gestapo with useful tips and find interesting contacts. Sitting together in the brewery pub these days are Josef Mayrlehner, Karl Hiebler, a Party functionary from Braunau known to both of them, and a civilian whom neither knows. In this locality, there is probably quite a lot of illegal radio-listening going on, volunteers the stranger, apparently casually, and Karl Hiebler says what he knows about this or that person and their preference for enemy radio stations.

Let's not forget that even Karl is only a human being. He repeatedly has the unpleasant task of going from door to door with collection boxes for donations to the People's Welfare, the Red Cross, and numerous other charitable institutions. When someone like Anna Mühlinger then begins to kick up a dreadful fuss about Hitler and the Nazis who are to blame that our lads are at the front, the exemplary idealist first tries to explain that the donation is also for the benefit of her brother on the battlefield. Hiebler really isn't prepared for this factual comment, which makes the woman's blood boil even more. *I was very depressed about the Mühlinger woman's moaning because I was giving up my Sunday and had to listen to things like that.* Is it then any wonder that it warms the cockles of your heart when a complete stranger takes time in the pub to listen patiently to everything that you're suppressing day in and day out? Karl Hiebler is grateful, and the Gestapo is also grateful. Anna Mühlinger is allowed to reflect on her insensitive behavior for a while in prison.

Vladimir Bezdek is strictly barred from receiving or writing letters. The Regional Commissioner for Labor Education, Senior SA Major Franz Kubinger (we've unjustly almost forgotten him) is indeed making large-scale provision for new stocks of exploitable human resources. But in general, he is only moderately interested in routine camp trivialities such as torturing and killing since in his eyes they are really only rounding off the broad spectrum of effective educational measures. In the particularly serious case of Bezdek, Kubinger does admittedly see an urgent need for action and issues the appropriate directive to Commandant August Staudinger in person: whatever happens, Vladimir's disgraceful German girlfriend, the dishonorable slut Maria Haider, must be prevented from communicating directly or indirectly with the prisoner, needless to add that such a complete ban on contact is not provided for either in the Gauleiter's decree or in the camp regulations. But for the sake of the purity of German blood, Franz Kubinger takes the responsibility for this arbitrary act as well.

Nevertheless, Vladimir Bezdek is a lucky fellow. One day, completely out of the blue, when hardly any of the sought-after places in the institution are available for fellow citizens in need of educating, and the relatively small number of men beaten to death is not exactly easing the precarious situation in the long term, the gentleman from Moravia receives a fantastic offer from Kubinger: it might be possible to talk about his immediate release if he were to commit himself in writing to leaving the Reich District of Oberdonau for good within the next twenty-four hours. Vladimir doesn't deliberate for long, signs, and is never seen again.

From now on, the singing lesson thus has to manage without choir member Vladimir. We may picture the scene as follows: Educator Josef Mayrlehner, a gifted amateur musician, acts as the conductor every evening at nine for half an hour, in front of him the crowd of prisoners devoted to singing, who after ten hard hours of work feel in the mood for cultural activity before going to sleep. Guard colleague Josef Wieger is leaning unobtrusively against the wall until the leader of the choir, angry about a false entrance or a note that has been sung flatter than stipulated, gives him a tip to this effect. Then Wieger leaps towards the sinner with his rubber truncheon, lands two or three blows to the back, and returns to his initial position. Start again: "Kein schöner Land in dieser Zeit" ["No More Beautiful Land at this Time"].

It is wet and inhospitable in late autumn. Clouds of mist drift over the building site on the Moosach. The prisoner Johann Enthammer remains stuck in the damp earth with his heavily laden wheelbarrow; he can go neither forwards nor backwards. Despite the cold, the sweat beads on his brow, not from exertion, but because he knows what's to follow: Josef Mayrlehner is already approaching briskly. Without any rhyme or reason, the rubber truncheon strikes down on its victim, who is soon lying there whimpering. Mayrlehner now gives the defenseless man well-aimed kicks and rolls his dirt-smeared body several meters, right up to the riverbank, as if dealing with a medium-thick tree trunk to be floated downstream. One more mighty kick, and Johann Enthammer will go under. His torturer raises his arm but doesn't strike. He heads off laughing.

Surrounded by such imaginative staff with a strong,

local, slightly coarse sense of humor, butcher August Staudinger is absolutely in his element as Camp Boss. He likes to tend to his charges' physical injuries in person, be they slight or severe. Especially after his work is over, when his thirst has been quenched, he always has a weakness for little jokes and sophisticated entertainment. It was a priceless idea, for instance, to sneak after midnight, shhhhh, into one of the prisoners' rooms, and shoot at the ceiling with his duty revolver, so that all of them fall out of their bunks in fright.

His mate Josef Mayrlehner is also famous for original midnight pranks in the dormitory. Not that he would completely neglect his hobby during the day; in fact, he's really fond of challenging people to commit suicide, the sort of thing that apparently excites him. That's why he is also the source of regular suggestions on the building site that people hang or drown themselves, which, however, presupposes a certain talent not given to everyone. That's why at the witching hour the good Josef actually creeps up with a rope to Edmund Haller's plank bed, wakes him roughly, and says in an imperious tone that he must come with him immediately and hang himself. Edmund Haller declines and begins to scream. Josef Mayrlehner withdraws disappointed.

In the hospitals in the surrounding area, people are a bit surprised when, as autumn arrives, followed as scheduled by winter, dozens of prisoners are admitted with third-degree hypothermia. That is, after all, the highest possible level on the scale, which doesn't stretch endlessly upwards. Mr. Ludwig Kriechbauer from Steyr, for example, only thirty-six years old and a bear of a man when he entered the camp, dies in his hospital bed one day before Christmas as a result of such exposure and because of his highly advanced general state of exhaustion, as it's diplomatically phrased. This dead body is covered as well with bloodstained welts. The weeks of beatings have turned him into a wreck.

But not much skill is needed to explain the critical frost damage: it's a matter of principle that the hard labor is performed professionally in light work clothes and without gloves, naturally even when the temperature's well below freezing. A river has to be regulated, and it may well come to pass that someone, by mistake, or at the instigation of the guard team, becomes pretty wet. A dry change of clothes is not provided. You might as well start to hand out umbrellas. These lazy so-and-sos aren't made of sugar after all. Further hardening is provided by the popular roll calls on the camp grounds. This often means standing at attention for half an hour with bare feet on a solid cover of snow. The consequences are commensurate.

The splendid chaps from the SA feel secure and on top of the world. For months everything has been going well. So the Regional Commissioner for Labor Education, Franz Kubinger, has really not promised too much. Everyone can celebrate to his heart's desire, and nothing happens – in a word, blissful conditions. For a long time now, the severely injured are being sent out to the surrounding hospitals of Salzburg, Laufen, and Braunau, from where they may return to the camp more or less patched up or – because of fatal consequences – may not. For anyone who kicks the bucket on the premises, the district doctor simply writes out a death certificate with as little detail as possible. Those who fall dead outside camp are interred without much ado in the local cemetery. Provision is made for well-nourished newcomers; the numbers are regularly replenished.

Out there in the moorland, work is progressing satisfactorily. For a long time now, the landscape has been showing signs everywhere of large-scale operations. Instead of meandering out of control through marshy meadows, the brownish-red, peaty river is now tamed between artificial river embankments of black earth, on which no fresh grass has yet grown. Gigantic granite blocks on both sides make it clear to the river: escaping is pointless. The huge building site is progressing well: new tracks are laid, old ones taken up. Seen from above and from some way off, it's teeming with activity, the very model of proper employment policy in the Third Reich, located virtually round the corner from the house where the Führer was born.

Officially, all admission applications pass across the Linz desk of Party Member Franz Kubinger. If explicitly relevant terms are found anywhere in them, like "asocial" or "unwilling to work," any further scrutiny is unnecessary in his opinion. There are other things to be done, after all. Of the nineteen special departments of the German Labor Front, two are already in his charge: construction and mining, and soon a third section, stones and earth, will join them. Over and above that, his hands are tied anyway by duty regulations. As a functionary of a Party Government Department, he's not permitted to ask the police for additional investigations. At least, that's how Franz will later innocently justify himself.

Soon it's known throughout the length and breadth of Oberdonau that admissions are running like clockwork. *It is strongly recommended that a few communities should join forces in order that the committal costs may be reduced.* The Gauleiter's decree turns out in practice to be nothing but a formal cover-up to eliminate the last remnants of public suspicion. The local government politicians and other office holders are thus becoming visibly bolder and exhausting the possibilities. The Sub-prefect of Gmunden, for example, no longer refers to those documents that officially regulate possible admissions to the camp and thus spares Franz Kubinger, the Regional Commissioner in charge, one entire application, solely by referring back to a Welfare Education regulation in order to get rid of young Joachim Buchinger. And it seems best do it by the direct route if it can be arranged. No problem, says August, our butcher. Let's have him.

When Dr. Eypeltauer, acting as deputy to his colleague, the Senior Public Prosecutor, gives a detailed report to the Reich Minister for Justice in Berlin many months later, he brings up further appalling cases. Johann Koller, eighteen years old, is one of them: *Not until later did police investigations reveal that there could be no question of being work-shy or an asocial element and that the Vöcklabruck branch of the Gmunden Employment Office had made its admission request without obtaining more background information about the man in question.*

Meanwhile, the intimidated, tortured prisoners in the hospitals have completely lost heart. They know nothing of camp regulations to which they could appeal. They have good reason to feel that they are fair game, with absolutely no rights at all, and often enough do not even know why. Of course, they describe the ordeals to doctors and nursing staff when requested, but their condition in any case speaks volumes. Yet at the same time, they wring their hands and ask that no doctor put the camp administrators on the spot; that would mean certain death for them.

Mayor Michael Kaltenberger makes a pretty good profit from the indescribable suffering of others. He, the forward-looking leaseholder of the whole area, demands for the camp grounds alone about fifty percent more from the District Welfare Authorities, the official subtenants, than he is prepared to pay the impoverished farmers, the Geratsdorfers, under the terms of the contract. There remains in addition the agricultural land, at least nine hectares of usable land, which the crafty NS-multi-functionary is also not farming himself but is leasing to other farmers. Up to now, however, as was to be expected, the promised investments in the substance of the buildings have not on the whole materialized.

On the evening of the twenty-second of December 1940 the St. Pantaleon NSDAP Local Group organized a German People's Christmas in the hall of the Kaltenberger pub. The *New Watch on the Inn* provides a comprehensive report: *At the center of the celebrations was the honoring of German mothers with the awarding of the Crosses of Honor for German mothers. The song "Great Night of the Clear Stars" opened the festive hour; there followed torch-lit recitation of verses by Hitler Youth, Junior Hitler Youth, and members of the League of German Girls. District Party Group Leader Comrade Kaltenberger spoke about the meaning of the German Christmas festival as the most beautiful festival for the German family and particularly honored, in heartfelt words of thanks and in recognition of her silent sacrificial fulfillment of her duty, the upholder of the German family, the German mother. The impressive hour of ceremony closed with the request to the Dear Lord to keep the Führer in good health for a long time to come and with the song "Sacred Fatherland."*

The next day – during these hours Ludwig Kriechbauer died an agonizing death in the nearby hospital in Laufen, and is no longer available – is the beginning of the end in the life of the freshly admitted prisoner Josef Mayer. By way of prelude, Camp Commandant August Staudinger bangs his fist into the face of the forty-one-year-old trained cobbler for no real reason, as it was his custom. When the Honorable Mayor enters his camp shortly after that, on what he calls his Christmas visit, he immediately notices Mayer's swollen face; he is wearing a plaster on the bridge of his nose. Mayor Kaltenberger then asks whether all the protégés are well. Nobody complains, everything is just fine.

Christmas Eve on the building site: Josef Mayer is

beaten so violently with a rubber cudgel that he falls to the ground. Towards midday, he drags himself bent double with back pains into the line again. Time to assemble for food – Josef is far too slow for the SA, and furthermore he isn't standing up really straight and at attention, as is right and proper. This new boy still has a lot to learn or his days will rapidly be over. He takes further beating until he falls down unconscious. The dashing Alois holds a pistol to his temple and threatens to press the trigger. Mayer no longer reacts and remains for the time being lying in the snow. Finally, the unconscious man is bundled off on a sledge and – they're closing a bit earlier than usual today in honor of the occasion – dragged home to the camp.

On Christmas Eve comes the climax of the holiday, a surprise for the inmates in the form of a distribution of gifts in the manner approved by the camp officials. Even before the modest evening supper, a large Christmas tree is erected. The guard staff have the prisoners fasten candles to it. There are also candles on the tables; today for once the services of the naked light bulbs will not be needed. After the meal, SA-Storm Leader Gottfried Haimbuchner delivers a short festive speech on behalf of the Camp Commandant. Unfortunately, in contrast to the day before yesterday, it is not only August Staudinger who is absent from this thoughtful celebration but also the *New Watch on the Inn*, and so we must go to the trouble of describing the important atmospheric images ourselves: in any case, the homely, warmly flickering candlelight bathes the grand Christmas beating in a mild, almost intimate light. Its inventor, Camp Director Staudinger, sends his apologies with a heavy heart, as does Josef Wieger. Both have taken a few days' leave during the festive period. Well briefed, Alois Rosenbichler, Gottfried Haimbuchner, and Josef Mayrlehner set to work.

About ten victims are selected, including what is left of

the prisoner Josef Mayer. Trousers down, one after another they're strapped naked onto a bench. Fellow-prisoners have to hold them down by the legs and head, so they can neither defend themselves nor evade the blows in any way. While the SA men are thrashing away like crazy at the naked bottoms, some victims have their mouths held shut with caps. They're simply screaming too loudly, and civilians in the neighborhood might even be disturbed during their Christmas carol singing. Meanwhile, Anna Schmiedinger, the temporary cook, is seeing to the washing-up next door in the kitchen. This time she's in a particular hurry, and that's for two understandable reasons: first, the noises from the dining room, as she'll later testify, are terrible to listen to, and second, she'd like to be back at home as soon as possible. After all, it is actually Christmas Eve.

This Mayer is a pretty tough lad and he survives this day as well. The whole of the following day he's left lying there; he scarcely moves. On Christmas night guard Alois pulls the disfigured body violently out of the top bunk. On his final rounds, it has in fact been reported to him by the dormitory prefect that Mayer's clothes weren't folded according to the regulations. Dazed and weak, Josef collapses. Rosenbichler pulls him by the hair into the middle of the room. Stand up, he's urged. Josef tries as hard as he can, crawls on all fours, supports himself by the frame of the plank bed, pulls himself up and finally stands on wobbly legs. Two or three massive blows with the rubber truncheon, and Josef is prostrate again. Stand up, he's urged. The little game is repeated at least ten times. This Alois has all the time in the world. Then the tortured man finally remains lying in blood and excrement, barely able to whimper. Senior Staff Sergeant Rosenbichler feels in excellent form today and considers the time has come to use his hobnailed boots to give the little heap of a man countless kicks in the genitals. Inarticulate sounds of pain are the consequence.

In total, the dedicated pedagogue is apparently occupied for a full hour until he has finally achieved his educational goal: Josef Mayer no longer utters a single sound. Fellow prisoners are instructed to lift him up by the arms and scrotum and heave the lump of flesh onto his bunk. Two or three hours later, Josef suddenly tumbles down from his bunk bed onto the floor and gets a further gaping wound on his head. Gottfried Haimbuchner now orders fellow prisoners to give him a makeshift wash, and put him on a regular plank bed. A further day elapses.

Early on the evening of St. Stephen's Day, the doctor makes his routine visit to the camp. As he's there already anyway, he's taken to see the dying Josef. With the best will in the world, there's nothing more that can be done for him. Nevertheless, Dr. Straffner immediately gives him a heart-strengthening injection, then discovers encrusted blood on the surface of the face over the right cheek and on the lower jaw, as well as blood in the eyeballs, bloodshot lower eyelids, and a bloody nose. In view of the man's moribund condition, the doctor doesn't bother to undress the patient. Josef still has almost the whole of the coming night to suffer. At four o'clock in the morning it's over.

The day afterward, almost all members of the St. Pantaleon Local Unit of the NSDAP are present for the social evening in the Brewery Pub in Wildshut. The first task is to listen both reverently and patiently to Michael Kaltenberger giving his comprehensive account of the year that has just ended. He pays particular tribute to the beneficial work of the German Labor Front, listing among other things the number of donations received by the Winter Relief Program and the War Relief Program of the German Red Cross, to wit, the fine sum of twelve thousand Reichsmarks; he emphasizes that the District

Party Group Management received no less than one thousand, two hundred calls from people seeking advice and help, that two hundred and nineteen letters from soldiers at the Front arrived at the Local Unit, and two hundred and thirty-one were sent from the Local Unit to soldiers at the Front. *During Christmas week, 240 field-post parcels were sent by the NS Women's League to our soldiers and in addition two knitted blankets.* After so many impressive figures, they're rewarded with several hours of a cozy, comradely get-together to see the old year out, reports the *New Watch*. Today the paper's there again.

Meanwhile, Josef Mayer is lying in the post-mortem room of the local mortuary. The autopsy will reveal wide areas of abrasions on both knees, lacerations on the buttocks, severe tissue bleeding of the scrotum, countless internal and external injuries from head to toe, as is recorded verbatim in the final autopsy report. The immediate cause of death is said to be concussion. It is certified officially that Mr. Mayer must have died a particularly painful death. He lived forty-one years and finally ends up in a grave in the local cemetery in St. Pantaleon.

Saint Pantaleon is one of the fourteen auxiliary saints. He's supposed to have been a famous doctor who healed the sick by virtue of his firm Christian beliefs. That's why he's often called on cases of injury to body and soul. His own martyrdom under Emperor Diocletian is recorded in detail and includes scourges, burning, and starvation before he was tied to an olive tree to be executed. The blow of the sword which was supposed to decapitate him was not directed with sufficient precision and split his skull. A silver reliquary bust of this patron saint of midwives and doctors is kept in the village's parish church. Miracles that could be attributed to the mediation of St. Pantaleon failed to materialize during these Christmas days in 1940.

Lost in thought, we allow our fingers to slide across the indentations of the one-shilling official stamp, which was needed to make Josef and Maria Mayer's wedding certificate lying before us now into an official document. On November 20, 1923, the daughter of the house owner Anton Schweiger thus consented to marry the son of the master shoemaker and house owner Theodor Mayer in Neukirchen, twenty kilometers from St. Pantaleon. On that occasion, both fathers acted as witnesses. We know nothing about the seventeen years of marriage, and the reasons for Mayer's admission to the camp are obscure. A removal of the body is not planned.

Oh yes, by coincidence, exactly half a year has passed since Franz Kubinger's good idea became reality. It has proved to be a sweeping success; it seems at the moment as though everything is running like clockwork. The SA has its fun, the Water Authority its cheap labor force, the intimidated victims slave away for dear life. Who knows, each morning may well be their last. *Special costs relating to education in the camp are deducted from wages.*

II

On December 28, 1940, I was notified in a telegram from the Wildshut District Court that the camp inmate Josef Mayer was found dead on Friday, December 27, 1940, in the Labor Education Camp in Weyer in the Administrative District of Braunau. According to a statement from the Camp Physician, there is a suspicion that death was by use of force.

That's how it begins, the clinical report by Ried's Senior Public Prosecutor, Dr. Josef Neuwirth, on the next to last day of the year. Franz Kubinger and his men feel they are absolutely safe. Not in their dreams do the stylish members of the Alpenland branch of the SA think about legal proceedings, let alone a judicial system that can't be intimidated, that begins to investigate meticulously without regard to persons or fear of the Party authorities or any other such anachronisms, long thought to belong to the past. So the dislodged avalanche hits them all the more unexpectedly.

Camp Physician Dr. Alois Straffner, himself a NSDAP member, Local Department Manager of the National Socialist People's Welfare and District Counselor in St. Pantaleon, has thus called in the authorities after all. He has long been familiar as an accessory and compliant recorder of more or less natural causes of death, as a physician who often supplies his colleagues in the hospitals with patients in terrible condition. He has to watch how the little SA Führers commit more and more monstrous atrocities from week to week because apparently nothing, even the most sadistic perversion, has any legal consequences. In the month of December alone, they've brutally murdered three men so far. Dr. Straffner has the choice of becoming more and more embroiled in these crimes every day or risking being discharged. The mortal remains of Josef Mayer, covered with torture scars, make the risk seem serious. They should start by explaining this condition. The doctor takes a deep breath, writes a factual account, and drives to the police station in Wildshut. We consider it pretty unlikely that he drops the internal bombshell a few hours later in the middle of the Christmas comradeship evening of the Nazi party.

While the Court Commission resumes its on-site work the very next day; while court physician Dr. Gerhardinger carries out the autopsy in the presence of his colleague Straffner, the Senior Public Prosecutor, the mayor, a police sergeant, and the local gravedigger; while Dr. Neuwirth announces he'll be instituting a preliminary examination on account of suspicion of the crime of manslaughter, alarm bells have long since been ringing for Senior SS Major Franz and Troop Leader August. The Camp Commandant does indeed notify the investigating officers in an imperious tone that he will on no account authorize police inquiries on the site he controls because Mayer merely had the misfortune of falling off his bunk in the night, but both of them quickly prepare themselves for a rearguard action.

The tortured, naked body of Josef Mayer quickly renders the group of mature and experienced men around the dissection table speechless. Above the bloodstained knees, testicles the size of pumpkins draw attention to themselves. One of the gentlemen finally breaks the silence, citing with some pathos the biblical phrase: Ecce homo! He says this in a low voice. Then it's quiet again. Awkwardly, they get down to work.

The diagnosis of exposure alone can be excluded with some degree of certainty as cause of death, is how the court physician sums up his findings and washes his hands.

Mayor Michael Kaltenberger seems the only one on whom it makes little impression; in fact, on the very day of the autopsy he is questioned about the matter and begins his report grandiosely, each word in the style of a Branch Group Leader of the NSDAP: *Because of my position of authority, I frequently visit the building site and thus have some insight into the human resources working there. You can already tell from the external appearance of the camp inmates that they have gotten out of hand and in their whole life have never taken much pleasure in work.* There was only one single time when he himself became witness to maltreatment, but probably there was a good reason for it. People had a low opinion of the camp, and in part rightly so, squirms Kaltenberger in response to detailed questions from the investigating officers. He succeeds for the moment in keeping secret how very involved he himself is, that he's making quite a tidy financial profit from the campsite of terror, and collecting the net rent as a secondary source of unearned income.

In their desperation and cowardice, the SA seeks refuge in the supposedly protective arms of the Nazi Party. They will indeed make earnest efforts to obstruct the investigations of the Criminal Investigation Department and to put the Public Prosecutor's Office under some political pressure. But Party Member Kubinger can say goodbye to his good idea. The news from the Linz parliament building is that he has overstepped the mark and is out of luck. The case is too hot. Now the NSDAP has to put the brakes on. First: the camp has to be completely evacuated within a week. Second: the stocks of files are, as far as available, to be handed in immediately to the District Authorities. Under no circumstances may they come into the hands of the Public Prosecutor.

Where are the prisoners to be sent then? asks the remorseful Franz sheepishly. Mauthausen is the lapidary answer; at least they can't open their mouths there. And the nice camp? Who will be doing the dirty work on the building site in the future? Or do the Party Members in charge perhaps want to cancel the ambitious and prestigious project without any further ado when it's only just got started? What's to become of the faithful SA mates from the Alpenland Branch? The Party thinks that all that should no longer be the concern of Franz Kubinger.

On January 9, 1941, prisoners and files did in fact disappear. Bigwigs from Linz proceeded in person to Weyer and ordered total evacuation. It all had to happen very swiftly, evidently too quickly to allow the much-invoked National Socialist thoroughness to prevail. The most important item found in the Camp Commandant's office is a seemingly overlooked list of medical insurance premiums, with one hundred and thirty-one prisoners' names, together with their dates of birth. The document proves to the Senior Public Prosecutor that, contrary to all the regulations, even sixteen- and seventeen-year-olds were given the dubious benefit of education.

The regular employees of the Water Cooperative are enlisted to sort things out within the abandoned camp. They won't forget in a hurry what they see there. But for the time being they merely remain silent. Fifteen to twenty delinquents lived in each so-called room. Their bedclothes are still lying around. The excrement, pus, and blood stains on many of the coarse, linen sheets over stinking straw mattresses speak for themselves. There are splashes of blood in the hall and in the cellar.

The Criminal Police hand over the delicate case to the Gestapo. These people are professionals and soon really do find forgotten, knocked-about prisoners in the surrounding hospitals, who report astounding things. Not only did sheer lawlessness evidently reign inside the walls of the camp and on the building site, but the circumstances of the admissions were, to put it mildly, highly dubious. During those days, the Public Prosecutor's Office in Ried in the Inn District, alongside the dreaded Gestapo, is very busy investigating Nazi crimes of violence, something which isn't an everyday occurrence.

Meanwhile, the Linz offices of the Oberdonau NSDAP are also working very hard. Outwardly, of course, normality and composure are expected; the regional administration's idea is that the camp should be populated again as quickly as possible. In the future, extra police and gendarmes instead of the halfwits from the Brown Shirt faction will be assigned to take care of the new inmates. Only Camp Manager Gottfried Haimbuchner is allowed to stay.

Over a year ago, Reinhard Heydrich, Head of the Security Service of the SS, on orders from the SS Reich Leader Heinrich Himmler, sent out a secret Express letter that was also delivered to the Party Members in Linz. Consequently, from October 1939 on, no Gypsies or Gypsy half-castes were allowed to leave their current place of residence. The decree from the Reich Main Security Administration describes them all without exception as work-shy and asocial. So their ceaseless roaming around came to an end. Racial researchers and Nazi ideologues, for practical rather than strictly scientific reasons, generously agreed, not as in the case of the Jews, on defining those people as Gypsy half-castes who had at least one-eighth Gypsy blood in them. One Romany great-grandmother is sufficient, so that even seven direct German-blooded ancestors are unfortunately unable to make any difference.

Half a year ago, the minors Vinzenz, Josef, and Amalia Blach were still playing in the Bad Ischl lodgings of their grandmother Aloisia. In the months of June and July, Mrs. Blach was twice summoned to provide information about her family circumstances to Ischl District Court, which was responsible for the guardianship. Aloisia Blach appeared very worried; her grandchildren had never before caused her to have any dealings with the court. She explained truthfully that she'd been providing board and lodging for the children of her unmarried daughter Maria since they were born and in response to related questions, assured the court that she also wanted to continue to do this. Her intention did not, however, tally at all with the still secret plans of the authorities. Two months ago, the Gypsy rabble in the whole of the Reich District of Oberdonau, with a few negligible exceptions, had been taken into safe-keeping as a preventive measure. Why not get them out of the hovels and put the fine ladies and gentlemen into the embarrassingly empty camp? Perhaps some of them can even be taught to work properly before they're disposed of − no sooner said than done.

On the nineteenth of January 1941, more than three hundred Sinti and Roma move into the new detention camp in Weyer. A whole ten days have elapsed since it had hastily been abandoned. A year later not one of these people will still be alive. But we've not got that far yet. This time there are many women among them, and half of them are children; that makes a colorful picture. Maria Blach is also in the convoy, and leaning against her is her eight-year-old daughter Amalia, whom we recognize beyond a doubt. They're all feeling pretty cold, we think; hopefully, they'll soon be assigned their sleeping places. The Gypsies who are fit for work quickly become acquainted with the building site in the midst of winter.

We have no records of how the capacity of the camp could be increased almost fivefold within just a few days. At any rate, St. Pantaleon's population grew instantly by just under a third. Whereas seventy percent are distributed comfortably over twenty-six square kilometers of district land, the remaining thirty percent have to make do with just a few thousand square meters. Are there really hundreds of new sleeping places ready in Weyer, could so many people be fed daily by the kitchen of the former pub even if you assume that only very simple dishes were prepared? What are the sanitary facilities like, and is it even possible to heat sections of buildings that were never before used as living spaces? Such peripheral questions didn't come up at the next session of the District Council. There's not – at least in the official minutes – any mention of the many new female and male citizens of Gypsy origin and of the dramatic events that took place in the camp before the turn of the year. Instead, the maintenance work on the district roads is up for discussion this time, not to mention the prompt formation of cattle-breeding cooperatives in response to the new Reich Animal Breeding Law.

Yet the new Gypsy Camp was a much greater worry for Mayor Michael Kaltenberger personally than it was for his fellow members in the Council. Admittedly, his reservations were completely different from our own. He studies the lease contract with the help of an expert, and discovers that his suspicion was only too well founded; the legal argument is unambiguous. With the best will in the world, the present use of the property can't be passed off as a continuation of the original one. The period of notice had thus begun with the closing of the Labor Education Camp. If the owner Geratsdorfer insists on it, the whole property is to be returned to them by the first of September of this year. This really goes against the grain, as far as the mayor is concerned. He has two reasons: first of all he would lose out on an attractive supplementary income, and on the other hand – and this carries significantly more weight – he has to some extent already maneuvered himself into a somewhat tricky position with the regional administration after the tiresome events of last Christmas. The possibility can't be ruled out that he'll have to step in front of the high-ranking gentlemen and confess that they're unfortunately going to be out on the street again from autumn onwards with their few hundred Gypsies. Kaltenberger will have to come up with something.

Despite all the difficult setbacks and exceptionally uncertain future of the River Regulation Project and the camp, the Honorable Mayor was determined to carry on. In fact, on the thirtieth of January, he sits down and writes a letter to the Senior State Court President in Linz inquiring what they think of his latest plan. In October 1939, the Wildshut prison in the district of St. Pantaleon, which was affiliated with the District Court, had, unfortunately, been shut down for reasons of cost efficiency. The fact that the cells were now to continue to stand empty is of great concern to the Head of the District, which is why he wishes the appropriate authorities to fill them with prisoners of war, with Frenchmen, to be precise.

Even letters that are subject to the strict rules of bureaucratic judiciary style can at times express bewilderment. The Honorable President's response proves this. In it, he says that neither the condition nor the proposed use of the rooms seemed advisable; furthermore, the proposed nature of the accommodation conflicted with the international *treaty of October 18, 1907, regarding the laws and conventions of land warfare.* Michael Kaltenberger is bitterly disappointed and amuses the State Court President with an unintentionally comic excuse when he responds, *with reference to your above-mentioned disclosure, I withdraw my proposal made earlier for housing prisoners in the local accommodation.*

Dr. Josef Neuwirth takes no notice of all of that and has little reason to laugh. In the course of those days, the vestiges of that camp which he is investigating are removed by the regional administration as well as possible. It is a race against time. The Senior Public Prosecutor rightly suspects that the doctored admission files are hidden away with the NSDAP District Leadership in Braunau and demands to see them. District Leadership seeks headquarters' advice from a close friend during the glorious years of illegality. Regional Inspector Stefan Schachermayr, the Gauleiter's right-hand man, responsible for personnel matters, petitions, queries, and complaints, is an ambiguous figure. Still young, the trained baker has already managed to get his own Stefan Schachermayr Street named after him in Braunau. How did that come about? Well, he once performed really heroic deeds as sales manager of the *Austrian Observer*, the inflammatory Nazi publication banned in the Austrian Corporate State. He conveyed the completed manuscripts from editor August Eigruber to the Braunau printing firm of Reithofer, the illegal District Leader. They then had to get the completed newspaper to the distributors in the various towns, an impressive thirty thousand copies twice a week, of which no small number found their way as far as Vienna and Salzburg – no problem for a real man like Stefan Schachermayr.

Shortly after the *Anschluss*, comrade Fritz Reithofer even had a street named after him, though he was barely twenty-seven years old, and he now proves himself to be also worthy of this special honor by taking up a strong pro-Fritz stance and striking out in writing. And thus Dr. Neuwirth learns unequivocally: *Your request that we disclose the names of all those people who were admitted in the above-mentioned period of time cannot be linked in any way to the investigation going on at the moment into alleged homicide. Therefore, the only conclusion which can be reached is that the Public Prosecutor's Office wishes to review the legality of all applications for admission to the camp that were approved by order of the Gauleiter and Reich Governor.*

It is in my opinion completely absurd that the Public

Prosecutor's Office should question the legality of measures taken by the Administrative Authorities or Party Headquarters.
Heil Hitler!

The Public Prosecutor sees things differently. He reads with a smirk that the good Regional Inspector has, by way of precaution, sent a carbon copy of his strongly worded response to the Linz Attorney General. But the latter has understood the situation for a long time and doesn't, although himself a member of the NSDAP, give a damn about the now-established legal perspective of the Party. He has the admission files sent to him, as far as they still exist, via the appropriate mayors, District Chairmen of the German Labor Front, Sub-prefects, and diverse other authorized people, who have cheerfully and assiduously availed themselves of this useful facility, a Labor Education Camp.

Just two weeks later the Senior Public Prosecutor for the first time reports to the Reich Minister for Justice in Berlin, via the Attorney General. On twenty-five closely written pages, he recounts the history of the camp, describing laconically what the questioning of the accused and witnesses has yielded up to this point; no gruesome detail is left out. He particularly emphasizes that young people were imprisoned in the camp against the express wording of the decree; the youngest ones were only sixteen. The Linz Attorney General sets all wheels in motion to get the underage prisoners out of the dreaded concentration camp in Mauthausen, since even their mere admission to the Labor Education Camp was not, according to his interpretation of the law, admissible. With regard to Mauthausen, the Reich Ministry of Justice, somewhat puzzled about it, learns from the report on the proceedings that Dr. Neuwirth considers it necessary to question fifty-one witnesses from Weyer in Mauthausen. There's also a transcript of the Regional Inspector's tirade, about whose defense the Public Prosecutor comments dryly: *No further elaboration is required of the fact that a Party Office is* not *authorized to carry out such far-reaching measures, which, like the admissions, do in fact represent an act of state sovereignty.*

That is shocking and unbelievable. In the middle of February 1941, in the middle of the World War, in the middle of the Third Reich, a subordinate agent of justice insists on the consistent separation of state and Party. But that is by no means everything. The Ministry of Justice discovers also that Alois Rosenbichler and Josef Mayrlehner had already been detained awaiting trial, and the arrest warrant for Camp Director August Staudinger was about to be issued. Regional Commissioner Franz Kubinger and even Regional Inspector Stefan Schachermayr were drawn into the investigations, whether as witnesses or as accused was not yet clear. Appropriately, as Dr. Neuwirth formulates it, but not without ulterior motives, he will in this matter avail himself of Gestapo officials as helpers. End of story.

Oh yes, one more thing. The Mauthausen Camp Commandant doesn't want to let him in to see the people requested as witnesses. The man is invoking regulations that he, the petty Public Prosecutor from the introspective little town of Ried in the Inn District, unfortunately cannot take into consideration. His question therefore to Berlin is whether authorization by the Reich Leader is really necessary here. A response is requested.

One week later, on behalf of Dr. Köllinger, the Attorney General, his deputy, Dr. Eypeltauer adds his bit of pressure. He informs the Reich Minister for Justice with satisfaction that in the meantime twenty-seven former inmates of the Weyer camp have been discharged from Mauthausen concentration camp. The Gestapo has asked for their addresses and will question them at their earliest convenience. Furthermore, they are starting immediately on the exhumation of the other corpses and their examination by Court doctors from Vienna. In other matters he subscribes to colleague Neuwirth's view and even says that the Regional Commissioner for Labor Education has been guilty in the intervening period of further offenses because he has forbidden former SA camp personnel to testify to the Gestapo. Mayor Michael Kaltenberger had also forbidden the SA guards from accounting for themselves to the Gestapo and would without a doubt have to be accused of that crime according to §214 of the Penal Code.

Admittedly, Kaltenberger still imagines he's reasonably safe, thanks to his many back-up options. The pub cinema in the village, for example, regularly provides a pretty decent income. As far as the first weeks of the new year are concerned, we can refer particularly to the completely sold-out performances of popular films by the German UFA Cinema Company such as *Mother-Love* and *Home-Country*. Veit Harlan's *Jew Süss* had probably already found its way into even the most remote provincial cinema halls and was surely an eye-opener for great numbers of cinemagoers.

Frau Amalia Göschl practises the fine profession of midwifery. She's used to irregular working hours. It therefore doesn't bother her, even late at night, to be called out because labor pains have set in somewhere or other. What's considerably less pleasant is the rumor-ridden neighborhood to which a policeman calls her for the first time today: the Gypsy Detention Camp, Weyer. For twenty-two-year-old Mathilde Leimberger, it's her first birth, and fortunately it proceeds without any great complications. In the official entry about baby Maria's birth, there is, incidentally, under the heading "last domicile" of the parents, just the curt: *Gravel pit in Traun near Linz*.

On the fifth of March, 1941, the forty-one-year-old electrical technician August Rössler is summoned to appear as a witness. A fortnight ago he was discharged from Mauthausen concentration camp; a year later he's to perish in Dachau concentration camp. Mr. Rössler gives a comprehensive statement, and even shows his frostbite scars. *I would finally like to mention that I am still owed my wages for ten weeks, that is, the wages up to my admission to the hospital. Storm Leader Haimbuchner received my wages from the Water Board but only paid me 3 Reichsmarks on four occasions as pocket money. On my admission to the camp, moreover, Camp Director Staudinger took my German Labor Front book, together with certificates of residence and baptism from my parents and myself, exam certificates, and other documents. These documents were never returned and I know they were not handed over to Mauthausen either, since I inquired there specially. The stamps for 2½ years are in the German Labor Front book, and I would have to buy replacements for all of them.*

SA Storm Leader Gottfried Haimbuchner was one of those people who likes to keep himself in the background. Rumors were already circulating that the financial irregularities in the Weyer camp under his stewardship were running to a total of several thousand Reichsmarks. Whatever the case, Haimbuchner soon admits that he too has been diligent in thrashing people. During the Christmas punishments, for example, as he can suddenly remember after all, he took on Edmund Haller and gave him twenty-five rubber truncheon blows to the buttocks. But, and Gottfried lays very great store by this, nobody was killed in the process.

During these weeks under SA Storm Leader Gottfried Haimbuchner's reliable supervision, people were admittedly again dying in the new camp. The inmates at the moment had the misfortune not to be Aryan. That is to say, when Heinrich Himmler in 1942 has serious reservations on account of the latest racial hygiene advice about Gypsy-like persons, wondering whether they were not in fact actually dealing with descendants of Indo-Germanic, that is, Aryan, ancient people, and temporarily halted the annihilation of the Roma and Sinti, it's a few months too late for these people in this camp. Anyone who's unlucky and fortunate has already died by now.

Dr. Straffner is officially playing the role of Camp Physician again, but he has decidedly less work than before despite the fact that the number of internees has multiplied. We don't want to come to any premature conclusions and aren't rejoicing too early that the conditions in Weyer have become decidedly more civilized: it's simply because the interned Gypsy rabble have no medical insurance, and for this understandable reason, they are not entitled to decent medical care. In fact, the new people in the camp are mostly treated in official documents as a grey, faceless mass. They hardly appear at all as individuals unless they are born there, formally put in the care of a guardian, or pass away. But even that will change.

At the inconspicuous address of Weyer Number Six, death has been a constant guest since the early part of the year, probably just a coincidence. In the parish Register of Deaths the camp victims are found entered peacefully alongside the fifteen to twenty village deaths that the calendar year normally brings. Each man and woman who dies merits a whole page regardless of standing, and Michael Kaltenberger duly signs, in his function as Registrar. In the case of those sentenced to the Labor Education Institution on racial grounds who have since passed away, Dr. Straffner signed the following note only a few weeks earlier: *Entered according to the report of district physician Dr. Alois Straffner. The man reporting this is known to the Registrar and explains that he knows about the fatality in his professional capacity.* Attached was the cause of death, described in appropriately specialist terminology. *Comotio cerebri or brain damage*, is how it reads, for example.

Today there's once again a nice neat entry in the Register of Deaths: *residing in St. Pantaleon, Weyer Number 6*. After all that has happened, however, Michael Kaltenberger does not lay any great store by Dr. Straffner's services as witness. The diagnosis for the dead Gypsy child Rudolf Haas is provided this time by Storm Leader Gottfried Haimbuchner, who is, because of the relatively lighter burden of detention while awaiting trial, temporarily the only remaining official in the camp of the old Alpenland Branch of the SA. *Too weak to live* is what they jointly enter as the cause of death, these two dreadful gentlemen, too weak to live! They aren't familiar with a Latin equivalent. Unfortunately, they have to make do without one.

One day later, the district doctor routinely and half-heartedly dashes off the formal certification of death: 1. First and family names (in the case of children under 14 years the occupation and name of the parents or the unmarried mother is to be declared): Haas Rudolf. 2. Gender: male. 3. Date and place of birth: April 8, 1941. 4. Day and hour of death: May 5, 1941, 15.30. 5. Occupation: (in the case of wives, the husband's; in the case of children, the father's): Gypsy. 6. Domicile: (town, street, house number): Weyr Nr. 6. 7. Town, street, and house number where death occurred: Weyr Nr. 6. 8. Day and hour of the inspection of the dead body: May 6, 1941, 15.30. 9. Cause of death: Too weak to live. (a) Underlying disease?: /. (b) Concomitant illnesses?: /. c) Subsequent illnesses: /. d) Which of the previously mentioned conditions was the direct cause of death?: /. e) Name of the doctor who officiated (legible): /. f) Any treatment other than by a doctor and by whom: /. 10. Are there any signs of an infectious disease present and if so, which?: no. 11. Are there any signs present of an unnatural death and if so, which?: no. 12. In the case of children under 1 year: a) type of feeding: mother's milk. b) whether being cared for by a third party: /. c) if the answer to b) is Yes, by whom: /. d) Are there any signs of severe neglect? /. 13. Has the dead man/woman a) been treated by the signatory doctor?: no. b) or been known to him?: yes.

In this respect at any rate, the calculated risk taken by the Party is completely successful: because the events in and around the Labor Education Camp have at least once been scrutinized most carefully by the judiciary, not one person in the next sixty years will concentrate on the Romany Camp long enough for there to be talk anywhere at all of little Rudolf Haas and the possible suspicious circumstances of his premature passing. Actually, apart from one solitary historian, hardly anybody at all deals with it, not the Public Prosecutor's Office of the Third Reich nor that of the Republic of Austria, not the district of St. Pantaleon, not the federal state of Upper Austria, and sensitive individuals who had to behold the misery themselves will probably only deal with it in their dreams.

Whether people like it or not, Rudolf is a child of this community. Born behind camp walls and barbed wire, he probably spends his short life in unsightly scraps of clothing lying on straw. It's fitting that his parents are called Maria and Josef; the mother came into the world twenty years previously in Salzburg-Maxglan, the father, eight years older, is originally from Westphalia. Now they're both residing in Weyer. The Register of Deaths does actually prove that the son of the couple is Catholic, so you can imagine how a man of the Church lifts up his cassock when he crosses the muddy dilapidated floor of the camp at the start of April to receive the baby at its mother's bosom into the community of believers. Perhaps he also comes back again in May to administer extreme unction when it's needed, but let's not forget that the priests in this area themselves spend a lot of time in the prisons. For inexplicable reasons, the dead Romanies, despite having the same home address as their dead fellow prisoners, are not buried in the cemetery in St. Pantaleon but in that of the neighboring village of Haigermoos, which was once compulsorily incorporated into St. Pantaleon. It's not very likely that Josef and Maria are permitted to witness the burial, even under supervision.

In yet another cemetery, this time in Laufen on the river Salzach in Upper Bavaria, a good ten kilometers away, a respectably dressed gentleman is having a discussion with the gravedigger. Senior Public Prosecutor Dr. Neuwirth has taken the long journey in person to examine the local requirements for the requested exhumations. He's looking for the graves of Messrs. Ennsthaler and Kriechbauer who succumbed to their severe injuries in the local hospital. Although both were buried only the previous year, the cemetery administration can unfortunately, even with the best will in the world, no longer give the location of the graves. That seems curious. Even the gravedigger, with whom Dr. Neuwirth paces around the fresh graves, is surprisingly ignorant

In the meantime, the interrogation of witnesses continues. Dozens of transcripts have already been presented to the court, including statements from many permanent civilian employees of the Water Authority, who now have to work with the Sinti and Roma, whom most despise. The detailed accounts tally on all the fundamental points. What's also becoming quite clear is that the guards were quick to use not only rubber truncheons but also service revolvers. Valentin Pfaffinger, for example, reports how the two Josefs in particular, Mayrlehner and Wieger, constantly aimed shots from a central spot, where they were resting on the building site, at the prisoners just beyond them who were slogging away too slowly. Their aim was to hurry them up. In this way, they apparently wanted to save themselves the trouble of getting up on their feet. With the detonations ringing in their ears, even the permanent workers never felt safe.

August Staudinger, once a butcher and farm worker, former Camp Director, now an accused, and to be in a few weeks a sapper at the front, begins meanwhile to speak his mind. He feels abandoned and seeks an escape route, even though in relaxed fashion. In the first instance he is concerned primarily to shed ultimate responsibility for the activities of his team. Officially, he explains, the disciplinary measures in the camp were a ban on smoking and deprivation of meals but not physical chastisement. The camp regulations themselves are unfortunately no longer in his possession, no, nor any copy thereof; Regional Inspector Schachermayr in person has taken the documents away.

The true villain is, however, without the shadow of a doubt, Franz Kubinger, August grumbles angrily. He was the one after all who introduced the orgies of physical punishment. Everything's covered, even possible killings, Kubinger continued when I asked him about it specifically. And now this, now we're supposed to be the morons. He wants to wash his hands of it, the fine gentleman, because of course he hasn't given it to us in writing.

Tangible proof is in pretty short supply at the moment. Admittedly, Alois Rosenbichler's hobnailed hiking boots can be seized. But the rubber truncheons (the criminal Josef Wieger delivered them privately, as he had the Alsatians) are unfortunately no longer available. Where are they? Some are burned; August shrugs his shoulders regretfully; the honorable Regional Inspector himself demanded that they be handed over.

He did certainly shoot frequently, Senior Troop Leader Josef Wieger now also vaguely remembers; he didn't want to deny that at all. But the shots were always fired to one side of the prisoners. Nor did he want to intimidate the latter, oh God, no. But they were new, the pistols, and the good man just had to break them in.

Yes, yes, he did invite various prisoners to kill themselves; that's certainly correct, but of course only as a joke, is how Troop Leader Josef Mayrlehner accounts for his actions. If they did in fact hang themselves or went into the water, that must be put down to the fact that they couldn't understand it was a joke.

Senior Staff Sergeant Alois Rosenbichler doesn't understand the world any more either. He reminds us that all the inmates were, after all, racial vermin. Then the bigwigs from Linz drove up and made detailed education proposals: by all means tie them to the trees, for example, and give them a proper beating, that was exactly what they said. As for the official camp regulations, you can certainly forget them, even after Christmas Regional Inspector Stefan Schachermayr promised on his honor that everything was covered. If you can't even trust the highest Party functionaries, then you're in a bad way.

The Public Prosecutor is pretty happy. There's no trace left of the wall of silence. All the SA Führer dwarves, who've been shrinking alarmingly for weeks, want now is first and foremost to save their own necks. They've recognized the seriousness of the situation, are incriminating each other to the best of their powers, and for this reason even divulge scandalous internal matters that add to the weight of the judiciary, compared to the apparently omnipotent but considerably sullied District Party apparatus. Each new transcript of an accused person's testimony makes Dr. Neuwirth a bit more confident.

The District Court in Bad Ischl transfers the guardianship of the under-age Gypsy girl Amalia Blach for logistical reasons to the Wildshut District Court. That's just routine work for judge Dr. Kotzmann, who has conscientiously been doing his duty since 1912, no matter who has been in power. The eight-year-old ward of the court is turned over to the District Youth Service in Braunau on the Inn and assigned an official guardian in nearby Ostermiething. It is almost definitely the case that this gentleman is doing nothing in the interest of his charge. Not one line, not even a tiny portion of a file can be substantiated. Yet no one, as has grudgingly to be recognized, can be accused of not following the rules.

We also leaf through other personnel files of interned Roma and Sinti to which we have access, read names, ages, places of birth: a certain Theresia Kerndlbacher, eighteen years old, from Natternbach near Grieskirchen is among them and her twenty-two-year-old partner, Hermann Kugler by name; moreover, Mathilde Leimberger, twenty-two, from Mühldorf on the Inn and her friend of the same age, Josef Lichtenberger from Pfarrkirchen. Who could even suspect that these people with their familiar-sounding names and places of birth were all stateless? The Nazi authorities are certain of it.

Castle Wildshut has a bloody legal tradition going back about a thousand years. According to the chronicles, most of the executions took place in the short time the curator Hieronymus, Baron of Metternich, held office. Roma and Sinti were affected. In fact, shortly after the Thirty Years War so many bands of Gypsies moved from Austria to Bavaria that they, together with their goods and chattels and all their relatives, were outlawed under the edict of February 19, 1658. With the collaboration of all the authorities, they were, as we read, rounded up everywhere, and those apprehended were, without a trial or judgment, executed by the sword, together with non-married women, their sons and their daughters, on Gallows Hill in Wildshut, right beside the Moosach river. The executioner's assistants then heaved the corpses straight into his carriage, headed for the nearby forest and buried them there. But children and young Gypsies up to the age of eighteen were exempted. They weren't murdered but were handed over to the peasants. In 1941 people are less soft-hearted on this point.

Maria Daniel is a born-and-bred Innviertel girl, as is her twenty-three-year-old mother from Handenberg. Just six years ago, this girl came into the world in Eggerding near Schärding on the Inn and was baptized a Roman Catholic. Her thick hair isn't blonde but rather so black that it shines bluish in the sun – wrong race, of course. One fine day in April, this child, interned in Weyer, is dead, that much is clear. Just one week before Camp Manager Gottfried Haimbuchner will announce that baby Rudolf Haas is too weak to live, the new Camp Administrator, Heinrich Neubauer, who as Head of the Criminal Police in Linz isn't exactly an expert in the finer points of medicine, diagnoses cardiac failure, according to the Register of Deaths, as the cause of death of little Maria Daniel. Mayor Kaltenberger sees no cause to doubt this diagnosis, and it's also quite possible that the two of them deliberated together for a little while about what they should settle on this time. At any rate, the spiky signature under the minutes does not betray any shaking.

So what broke the heart of young Maria? Exhaustion perhaps? Hunger? A mere chill, easy to get under control with warm tea and warm clothes but fatal in the damp, badly heated living quarters of the camp where even the bare essentials are missing? An injury, maltreatment? The conspiratorial certifiers believe, with some justification, that all clues have been obliterated. But they're wrong.

In his surgery at home, Dr. Alois Straffner fastidiously keeps records of his years of activity as coroner. Although he's not, according to the parish Register of Deaths, officially allowed to attest to the deaths registered in the camp, there's definitely material about them in his private documents – strange thing that. Even stranger, however, is the fact that Dr. Straffner thinks there's no doubt that little Maria died of so-called croup pneumonia, which, as older medical encyclopedias readily reveal, is generally attributed to severe damage caused by a cold. In contrast, the doctor has absolutely nothing at all to report about heart failure.

Are such inconsistencies relatively common? Comparisons with normal mortals show an extremely high degree of correlation between the medical coroner's diagnostic records and the parish Register of Deaths. Of course, just like everywhere else in the world, here too in St. Pantaleon there are little adjustments controlling the truth. If, for example, on the first of January in one of these war years, an expert opinion is to be passed on the death of a twenty-two-year-old person from the village, it may indeed be the case that the entry *Suicide* is heavily crossed out several times and the word *Poisoning* substituted.

But why different causes of death in the case of Maria Daniel? Let's speculate a little. Heart failure can't usually be foreseen, happens suddenly, and doesn't provide compelling grounds for nasty suspicions that a needy person has been refused adequate medical assistance. So was the fatally sick girl examined unofficially after all? Are the camp management and mayor rejecting what the doctor certifies in the Register of Deaths because they fear additional trouble if the real cause of the child's death comes to light? After all, Dr. Straffner, who continues to sit next to Michael Kaltenberger in the District Council, has already once attacked the latter from behind; after all, this Public Prosecutor from Ried is running things as though the Third Reich didn't exist.

For the sake of completeness, we consult Dr. Straffner's supplementary death certificate and find that in this third document a possible synthesis is attempted in a somewhat contrived way. He did indeed examine Maria when she was dying, the doctor confirms here, and he steadfastly maintains that her underlying disease was the aforementioned pneumonia. But then he gives the mayor and Camp Director a break after all, by writing under *9.d) Which of the previously mentioned conditions was the direct cause of death?* the words *Heart failure*, although he hasn't previously mentioned a possible heart condition anywhere. Oh well!

"Reich Minister for Justice" is printed on the letterhead of a communication that arrives at the Attorney General's office in Linz shortly after Maria's heart, for whatever reasons, ceased to beat. At the highest level, no fault is found with the procedures up to this point – quite the contrary. Dr. Schlegelberger, who was authorized to manage affairs in the Wilhelmstraße office in Berlin, had looked in detail at the thirty-one admissions files that had been transferred there and after scrutinizing them can imagine only too well how Stefan Schachermayr, the Regional NSDAP Inspector for Oberdonau, behaved in the dock, not to mention Senior SS Major Franz Kubinger. At the same time, the Ministerial Chancellery is, however, urging that the proceedings be speeded up. For this purpose, the Public Prosecutor was to limit himself for the moment to the fatal blows, the severe maltreatment, and the suspicious circumstances of the admissions. As far as the rest of the files relating to admissions are concerned, they were illegally confiscated by the Linz regional administration and so an investigation is necessary. *Since it is, however, not possible to count on their arriving in a short time, I request that in order to avoid any delay in the proceedings, the inquiry be conducted as far as possible without these files.* Ex-Camp Commandant August Staudinger was to be taken into custody as soon as possible. There is, however, not a single word in this letter about if and how the requested witnesses in Mauthausen concentration camp might be questioned.

The Ministry of Justice is apparently in a great rush. It may well be possible that they want to reach a legally binding verdict before the already noticeable interventions within the Party hierarchy have made their way right to the most sacred place, to Hitler's Reich Chancellery. It may well be possible that test cases like these are particularly suited for internal trials of strength between the Party and a judicial system that hasn't yet sunk everywhere to the level of the Freislerian People's Court. After all, the flagrant attacks on prisoners kept in Weyer camp occurred outside the domain of the near-omnipotent SS. In any case, the green light was given, and things began to happen.

In Oberdonau itself, people have not been inactive in the intervening period. The Gestapo, in this case on the side of the law, has questioned all accessible former prisoners after their release from Mauthausen. Some choose not to make a statement because they are understandably frightened, wriggle out of it, remain vague and tight-lipped; others speak out. Further facts that may be viewed as serious threats and physical violence are added to the files.

If one believes these witnesses, Senior Troop Leader Josef Wieger, for instance, must always have been in the habit of releasing the safety catch of his new duty pistol beside the temples of prisoners, precisely when the latter, incapable of standing up after being severely maltreated, are doubled over defenseless on the ground. In this regard, the survivors agree they recall Wieger's unflinching assurances that he will shoot them on the spot if they do not, for God's sake, stand to attention at once. Storm Leader Gottfried Haimbuchner, on the other hand, must have been so effective in holding onto the left ear of a prisoner during an educational session that finally he was holding a considerable part of the organ in his hand, separate from its owner.

The Senior Public Prosecutor summarizes these new findings in that first May week at precisely the time when Gottfried in his old domain convinces himself in his unchanged capacity as Deputy Camp Director that the dead Rudolf Haas was too weak to live and corrects the Camp records accordingly. Up until the end of the war, Haimbuchner remains to a large extent spared any appreciable unpleasantness. On the other hand, things get pretty hot for one Rosenbichler, Alois, and one Mayrlehner, Josef, his two SA comrades in detention awaiting trial. All official certificates in fact confirm unanimously and unambiguously the connection between their brutal maltreatment and the death of Josef Mayer.

In view of the overwhelming evidence, Senior Staff Sergeant Alois Rosenbichler no longer wishes to deny unequivocally the perhaps rather prolonged deployment of his hobnailed hiking boots in the area of the neck and genitals of unconscious torture victims. From that point on, his answer to the court is that he was firmly convinced, even though erroneously, that he was dealing with seasoned malingerers. Statements like this oblige Dr. Neuwirth to observe that the accused were deviously *attempting to lay the blame on camp inmates.*

Oberdonau Party bigwigs are in a state of great agitation, not that they feel so sorry for the careless Innviertel brown-shirt SA oafs, but the judiciary has worked its way up to the Regional Commissioner for Labor Education, a post invented by the Gauleiter. And if the investigation continues unhindered, Regional Inspector Schachermayr is also sooner or later a dead man. The next domino tile would be the boss himself.

Consequently, Gauleiter August Eigruber intervenes in person, draws on all his amassed authority, and summons the Attorney General to his house in the country. The latter, unshaken, outlines the state of the investigations in a businesslike way. That major criminal proceedings related to this matter are now only a matter of time is Dr. Köllinger's firm conviction, especially now that there has been a first case where forensic medicine could without a shadow of doubt prove the "fatal success" – to quote the German legal terminology – of the attacks by Rosenbichler and Mayrlehner. But of course that was only the tip of the iceberg.

Excellent, says Eigruber. Then the two men can be set free again. What was that? asks the Public Prosecutor. Well, the Gauleiter explains to his astonished counterpart, it keeps them from absconding or arranging to meet, and it may still be many months before the trial is held. Secretly, he is pretty sure that his friend Adolf will soon put an end to this absurd nuisance. Why let these SA idiots stew even longer; who knows what on earth the snivelling creatures will blab about if they have too much time in prison to brood? The Attorney General remains noncommittal, takes more time to consider, takes a deep breath for two weeks, and then drops in on the Gauleiter again. He lets him know that letting the two men out of prison is not an option.

SA stalwart August Staudinger is anxiously keeping himself posted, hoping in vain for a miraculous intervention by the Führer, and expecting to be arrested any day. Then the butcher suddenly remembers that a world war is going on and that for a long time now he has been feeling the irresistible urge to defend the fatherland in some distant place. Thus, the Public Prosecutor learns that it's unfortunately not possible, for military reasons, to issue the arrest warrant immediately, but it will, of course, be enforced as soon as the military situation permits it.

Not everybody has such understandable reasons as August Staudinger for looking forward to the Russian campaign that is about to start. Young men everywhere in Europe and beyond are volunteering in the name of the Führer, the nation, and the seven-year-old fatherland. Nobody asks whether they are doing this of their own free will; despite the censor, what they're really thinking is sometimes revealed in their letters: *Maridl, our son is now already one year old, and I can't see him. Now he'll be especially sweet and cuddly. As you write in your letters, he's already running all over the place. His parents should share his joy. Is he also already starting to speak? Maridl, when I get a chance, I'll send you money straight away so you can pay the nanny. Even though I can't be at home, my son and his mother are my greatest joy. Lately I've been having a really hard time, but now it's over, thank goodness, and I've survived. Maridl, now it's planting time. Maridl, on my next leave, we'll definitely get married.*

Sixty-four men from St. Pantaleon alone will die on the battlefield between 1939 and 1945. The regiment commandant will have to convey the bad tidings to parents and wives, and Maridl will not be spared this either. In 1950 dozens of veterans, Hitler fanatics as well as Nazi opponents, will be lumped together and be called intrepid heroes when the new war memorial is ceremoniously delivered to its destination. From then on, a life-size bronze soldier on the point of falling is given the unenviable task of delighting churchgoers, cemetery visitors, and primary school pupils from across the way as a reminder. Many participants in the war, however, prefer to stay away from veterans' activities for the rest of their lives, let others boast, and tell nobody about their nights bathed in sweat.

But let's not anticipate things any longer, for the already heralded hour has come for Pipsi and Mrs. XX. Pipsi is not a canary but a little dog, and Mrs. XX probably has a completely different name, but like all proper informers, doesn't want her full name to appear in the paper. Dog and mistress live in St. Pantaleon, as the *New Watch on the Inn* reports, and Pipsi is, according to the whimsical headline, a real detective. For days the animal refuses any food but is always terribly thirsty. Finally, Mrs. XX follows her little darling at a distance and witnesses how the dog pulls *a giant piece of salted meat out of the ground in the priest's garden*. The disgusted journalist writes that no further commentary is necessary in the light of these circumstances, which speak for themselves.

Mayor Kaltenberger has taken it upon himself to bring the activities of the priest to as rapid an end as possible. Since the last time the priest was released from prison, Kaltenberger watches over Johann Fuchs like a hawk, providing reports to the Gestapo at regular intervals. His links with the regional press are excellent; Kaltenberger is himself fond of supplying a news item now and then. And soon, with their combined efforts, they've actually managed it: the sickly churchman finally has to vacate the area and the parsonage.

But as feared, Michael Kaltenberger gets a cool reception from the Geratsdorfers. In the intervening period, they have learned that their apparent benefactor has well and truly deceived them. An extension to the lease is completely out of the question; they want their farm back. So the mayor agrees on a date with the District Farmers' Organization. He knows the people there and it really should be possible to arrange something. Well, it's not quite that simple, they advise him in Braunau. It will at the very least be necessary to work through the Donauland Regional Farmers' Organization. And we'll just do it through Vienna if it comes to that. Kaltenberger shows himself to be pugnacious: he is ready for a fight. But time is running out.

Maria Justina Müller comes into the world in Carinthia, when the current battlefield is called Königgrätz. It is the year 1866, and old Austria is just chalking up a devastating defeat by the Prussians. Thousands of dead bodies lie on both sides. Over the years, Mrs. Müller, known to all as Justi, has moved around a great deal in the new double monarchy of Austria-Hungary, which is already looking worn out again. On her family's extended expeditions, she soon learns that no joy is to be had from the vagrant Gypsies, even though for centuries the Romanies, together with Czechs and Hungarians, Slovenians and Ruthenians, Poles and Romanians, Jews and whoever else there may be, have made up the so-called multi-ethnic state. Maria's mother bore the pretty name of Rosalia, and even her mother was a subject of the long-reigning Emperor Franz, who restored the use of torture that his enlightened uncle Joseph had abolished. Justi has had a long life, and perhaps even outside the camp she would have died soon anyway.

In any case, because of her there's quite a lot of work again for the amateur doctors in the parish offices and the camp management. Detective Heinrich Neubauer certifies with his signature that the Gypsy Maria Justina Müller, aged seventy-five years, must without a shadow of doubt have succumbed to heart flesh degeneration. The mayor is extremely satisfied with this entry in the Register of Deaths, which somehow seems to be up to date; in his ears too, "heart flesh degeneration" sounds downright good.

We want to take this excellent opportunity to stress our appreciation that those people with Weyer Number Six as their address give the authorities administrative pleasure by passing away punctually on the hour or half hour, without exception. Through their cooperative demise, they thus save the Registrar from making onerous detailed entries under the rubric "minutes."

Two days before the beginning of the German offensive against the Soviet Union, the gravediggers of St. Pantaleon and Haigermoos rehearse an uprising together because, *according to §9 of the Inspecting Dead Bodies Regulation of 28.1.1855 in the Imperial Law Gazette, Nr. 210, every district chairman is obliged to appoint an individual for the purpose of providing assistance with the inspection.* They are these individuals. But a separate remuneration is envisaged for the performance of these duties. Now there have been times in which there was hardly anything in these matters that merited closer inspection; times are different now, however, and these duties are a tremendous strain for sensitive natures like theirs. That's why the autopsy assistants do not wish to forgo their supplementary allowances any longer. Mayor Michael Kaltenberger is, however, opposed to this modest request. So both the gentlemen immediately apply in person to the District Court responsible. Is there a mandatory rate for these services? they ask. Does the district, the state, or the court pay? Their petition is handed over to a higher authority.

A few weeks later, a Regional Court ruling is delivered to the honorable mayor. It states that it is unambiguously the duty of the district to provide extra remuneration for those who assist in inspecting the corpses. Of course, the district may initiate criminal proceedings against defendants whose cases being heard in court are related to the autopsy. At least in theory, the money in question could be paid out as compensation if a verdict of guilty is reached. At the moment, Michael Kaltenberger doesn't find this thought very funny.

Meanwhile, summer has moved into the land again. It is convenient that the higher temperatures are now appropriate for wearing the thin clothing with which most of the camp inmates have to make do. Senior Public Prosecutor Dr. Neuwirth from Ried in the Inn District has had his draft indictment typed out very neatly and sends off five copies by way of the Honorable Attorney General in Linz (Danube) to the Honorable Reich Minister for Justice in Berlin, W8, Wilhelmstrasse 65, not far from the Brandenburg Gate. What news is there?

According to the responses to the inquiries, three of the guards, as well as the Camp Director himself, must be charged with the crime of homicide, the crime of restriction of personal freedom, the crime of blackmail, the crime of making dangerous threats, and also the crime of attempted complicity in suicide in a trial to be held before the Senate of the Ried Regional Court in the Inn District. So writes the Public Prosecutor. In his opinion, no fewer than fifty-three witnesses and two experts are to be summoned.

Independently of this first charge a second bill of indictment goes off to Berlin for approval: Franz Kubinger, the Regional Commissioner for Labor Education, will probably have to answer to the court for the crime of complicity in an assault with a fatal outcome and the crime of complicity in blackmail. The grounds are detailed and unequivocal. The Public Prosecutor envisages as witnesses, among others, Mayor Kaltenberger and two SA Regiment Leaders of the Alpenland branch.

In the pages of the local Register of Deaths, Michael Kaltenberger, Registrar, states the applicable occupation before the name in the cases of men and women who are Aryan; there is, for example, a report about the unspectacular demise of the aged farmer Mathäus So-and-so, or about the dramatic end of an unmarried seamstress called Theresia, who, according to court reports, drowned in the very shallow Moosach as a result of shock, incidentally at a place where the prisoners were toiling in the immediate vicinity at the time in question. In front of the names of the dead Roma and Sinti, on the other hand, instead of a trade, there is simply the so-called racial affiliation.

In the village, everyone has extensive opportunities during these months to find their own individual image of the Gypsies confirmed. Some are frightened of the dark journeymen and professional criminals; others have romanticized ideas of a life with no ties, frivolity, exoticism, and deeply touching Gypsy tunes from operettas. Some feel in their powerlessness nothing but sympathy for these debased, disenfranchised people in the bleak adversity of the camp; others claim to have always known that they were dealing with unambiguously inferior human stock without whom they'd be better off.

When the Romany women and children have to help the farmers from the surrounding area with their harvest in their last summer, many Innviertel pigheads do not make use of them on grounds of principle because the rabble has no business on their farm or fields. Others integrate every potato hidden under a skirt during work into their own particular world view. There are furious complaints to the camp administrators that the Gypsies are pinching everything they can lay their hands on, but there are also natives of the area who secretly pass on food or some item of clothing to them. Administrator Gottfried Haimbuchner enters under income for 1941 in the *Gypsy Detention Camp Weyer-St. Pantaleon in the Reich District of Oberdonau* the sum of exactly one hundred and fifty Reichsmarks from work on farms and smallholdings.

The Attorney General's Office is busy in August clarifying to Berlin the bill of indictment issued by the colleague from Ried, placing special emphasis on refuting the impression that it was homicide only in the case of the prisoner Josef Mayer. They were optimistic that the reports would also lead compellingly to analogous conclusions in other cases. Quite apart from that, the fact that it was homicide was also clear because the guard who was obliged to ring a doctor immediately had, with hostile intent, failed to provide medical assistance. *If the trial is conducted in a suitably firm and energetic way, I do not doubt that in one or another further case those accused of homicide can be transferred.* And yet again the superlative-laden request for speed, speed, speed, this time from Linz: *I must, furthermore, point out that it is absolutely imperative that the bill of indictment be filed as early as possible because of the pressure from the Regional Administration to complete the criminal case as quickly as possible.*

The medic Dr. Straffner is at the same time the citizen Alois Straffner. He evidently likes taking photographs and does it exceedingly well; apparently, he goes in for new technological developments in a big way. He's just decided to set up some experiments with color negatives. He'll be able to project the resulting slides in giant format onto the living room wall. Alois Straffner, who has already had to see so much in this godforsaken camp, wants to see even more. His new theme is the Gypsies.

The sequence of visits with the camera is pure speculation, but this is how it might have been, if you want to trust the language of his pictures. There are hundreds of people all around, hardly any men, since they're likely to be on the building site. Some are leaning on brick walls, whose plaster is long since missing, while others are sitting directly on the brown, clay ground where no grass grows, getting through the days somehow or other. Let's imagine it's late afternoon; there are wispy clouds in the sky. There is evidently nothing here with which you could meaningfully occupy yourself, and of course no toys for the many little children. A lad clutches a horseshoe, an old woman with a knotted kerchief on her head has a cold pipe in her mouth. She immediately stands out, because almost all the people here are extremely young, average age at a guess seventeen, eighteen perhaps. Most are running around barefoot, some have worn-out, filthy shoes, rarely the right size. The clothes are shabby, baggy. But that's not what inhibits the guest; after all, farm laborers and maids don't look much smarter.

What he has to learn to deal with today is something completely different. He has stepped through the camp gate into an alien world and not as he normally does, as a doctor with clearly defined tasks, actively at work to administer treatment quickly, always in haste, with other patients at the back of his mind. On this particular day, he wants to engage with these marginalized people in their depressing point in time, just wants to quietly take a picture, indeed many pictures of them. Alois Straffner finds himself all of a sudden in an imaginary waiting room among countless wretched people who have dealings with one another, who belong together; even the first glimpse gives that away. They appear to the observer as if they came from far away, but when they open their mouths they all speak the local dialect like you and me, even if they often use a completely strange language among themselves. And they are, as an educated man like the district doctor is fully aware, herded together, confined, stuck here for no other reason than that they belong to the wrong ethnic group and because their customs and habits are no longer tolerated, habits which often are merely the result of centuries of stigmatization.

What is described in common derogatory parlance as "Gypsies roaming around" sounds, of course, quite different if you were for once to listen to these people and the terms they use themselves. If they speak about the time before they were detained, the phrase is: we were on our travels. They're not talking here about specific travels but about being on the road, about a way of life, and a dignity emanates from this formulation that allows one to measure what's being done to the Romanies when they're confined here in camps like this one. It's not the ground but the wheel under their feet that's been suddenly pulled away from them overnight. Of all the conceivable indignities that befall them in Weyer, this is without a doubt the most painful.

Does Dr. Straffner suspect after the dreadful experiences of the previous year that the country in which he lives has no use for the Romanies any more? Is the National Socialist Party Member aware that for a long time now Gypsies have also been interned in the large concentration camps? Is it true, as eyewitnesses attest to long after the war, that people in fact noticed tattooed prisoner numbers from Auschwitz in the case of some AG-GR (Asocial Gypsies, German Reich) and AG-St (Asocial Gypsies, stateless) interned in Weyer? Is Straffner perhaps even here to document an imminent nemesis, a thorough eradication, as it is now called? Is it this foreboding that makes him so timid? The Romanies also keep their distance to start with, appear mistrustful; with cautious curiosity many of the children eye the doctor-photographer and his expensive equipment. Alois Straffner begins to fiddle around with his tripod; he gets down to work.

In early autumn 1941, there are no longer any Jews to be found in the German army, but there still are Roma and Sinti. Their mere existence, as can easily be ascertained from an infinite chain of contradictions in the NS policy towards the Gypsies, overtaxes the schematic, inflexible, collectivistic, National Socialist state's image of society. Asocial *per definitionem* because they for the most part have no permanent place of abode, they are, on the one hand, not to be considered citizens of the Reich under any circumstances but on the other hand are unfortunately there. Even if the Nuremberg Laws manage without special directives concerning Roma and Sinti, only one year later it's stated in the commentary on German racial legislation that within Europe only Jews and Gypsies are of alien blood. That's already effectively half way to a death sentence.

It proves downright difficult to teach this spontaneously nomadic folk about the advantages of antlike bustling activity in files and marching rhythms. So it's soon considered necessary to set up a Reich Headquarters for "Combating the Gypsy Menace," and the decision is taken to regard Roma and Sinti as a plague, a visitation, just like the biblical locusts. And accordingly, the decree relating to this is given the handy title, "Fighting the Gypsy Plague." The German Reich wants to solve the problem on the basis of the nature of the race, as they put it in a formulation as spongy as it is threatening, but in the document it basically revolves around regulatory policy measures concerning all those elements who are traveling around, not holding down regular work, who are suspected of theft, who are a thorn in the flesh of those in power. It also, therefore, affects tramps and peddlers, regardless of what type of blood they happen to have.

Meanwhile, important men in white gowns, who have been raised by the Nazis to the status of anthropological specialists, tirelessly research and chart the topic of Romanies. The result is a veritable conflict of scholars. Whereas some calculate that the Gypsies have the moderate biochemical racial indicator of 0.6 – the Teuton may enjoy the rating 2.9 – and thus believe they've found objective proof of their inferiority, others feel the dreadful suspicion, if not the certainty, creeping up on them that they've identified ancient Aryan skull shapes.

In the midst of this pseudo-scientifically substantiated, infinitely cynical confusion, the policy also looks in practice as might be expected: on the one hand, up until July 1942, some Roma men who've foresworn their apparently innate roving spirit are standing in the battlefield and on Rear-Area service. On the other hand, at this moment thousands of Gypsies have long since been deported from the Reich to the *Generalgouvernement*, formerly independent Poland, and have been killed there, including all those interned in Weyer.

But right now they're still alive, and the private citizen Alois Straffner is just getting a group of eighteen Gypsy-like individuals into the sights of his camera. Only the children are looking at the lens; the adult women look down at the ground or to one side. The picture still suggests ample distance between photographer and object, and that's not just because of the technical details of the shot. The next scene: women are sitting with outstretched legs on the bare earth, children on their laps, children beside them. Behind them a dead tree. In a fork of a branch is a straw sack in a quilted cover – desolation.

We now, somewhat early, already have to make a short detour to Lackenbach in Burgenland. In contrast to Weyer, a relatively large number of Romanies in this detention camp will survive the Third Reich and be able to tell how they were treated. For the sake of its inmates, we want to hope that things were more comfortable in Weyer, but we can't really seriously believe that. Whatever the truth, Lackenbach in 1941 offers lousy food, inadequate medical treatment, overcrowding, lights out at eight p.m., and if required, beatings, blows with sticks, assignment to the cleaning of the latrines with bare hands. Yet there are cases of people being released, and with Himmler's newly awakened interest in Aryan traces in the Gypsy nuisance, the camp conditions even temporarily improve somewhat. Linguists come to visit and take samples of spoken Romany away with them; permission is given for modest parties with music, but by that time, the cremated remains of the last Weyer Gypsies have long since gone through the bone crusher.

One splendid day, Dr. Alois Straffner must have been in the camp one more time with his camera; the evening sun bathes the faces in a mild, forgiving light. The result is dozens of individual portraits and shots of couples and small groups: brothers and sisters, families, sweethearts, old married couples. The mood has completely changed. The resigned, ragged camp inmates from far away in the distance have become transformed into close acquaintances of the lens, and they've probably for one last time made themselves beautiful for someone who shows an interest in them, the debased, outcast, and isolated. Over thirty pictures survive; they show us attractive young people in mostly simple but clean clothes, men with neatly combed-back, thick hair, women with large earrings, and blouses and skirts printed with summer flowers and autumn leaves. A dashing young man is even wearing a pinstriped suit and a bow tie with his white shirt; a young mother is wearing her pearl necklace. Evidently, they hadn't yet had all their good garments taken away; the stuff was probably lying in suitcases and boxes and then handed out by the camp administration for this photo session by the honorable doctor who has no evil intentions and only innocently wants to document Gypsy Romanticism the way it's found in books.

May we really regard these images so naively? After all, Dr. Straffner does have a vital interest in later being able to prove that things were very different this time, and who'd be cross with him for this? Admittedly, some people are dying there again, but outside in the normal world, there's also a reaper whose name is death. Just look, is the message of these unique photographic documents; the people here are cheerful and happy; they're short of nothing in this camp; at any rate, I, Alois Straffner, wash my hands in innocence. Sixty years later, the photos will still serve as proof of the institution's sanitorium-like quality for those who prefer to believe the fascinating, old, but obviously staged, color photographs and trust the orally transmitted, watered-down stories rather than the original written documents.

Alois Straffner has sought out a particularly decorative background; he places most of his subjects, one after another, in front of the same piece of wall from which the plaster has long since crumbled. And as a matter of fact, the warm evening red of the bricks, the golden yellow skin of these people in the light of the low sun, the shining dark hair and their unaffected cheerfulness, whatever may have inspired it, give these photos an unreal, relaxed, optimistic feeling of peace. From somewhere or other, a girl, perhaps eighteen years old, has even got hold of high-heeled shoes, and there she is posing now, hands on her hips, nestling against a girlfriend, proud, self-assured, ready for all that life has to offer. They're all touching one another; is *tender* the word? They've put their heads together, their arms around one another's shoulders, so one might think that they're embracing one another, holding each other tight, in order not to go astray.

The date is the fourth of September, 1941. Today, in Vienna's Löwelstraße, the headquarters of the Donauland Regional Farmers' Organization, (Reich Agricultural Organization, Subsection: Blood and Soil), an illuminating document is being dictated in the name of the Director of the Regional Farmers' Organization. In it, an application is made to the Agricultural Court to allow the property of the husband and wife Max and Maria Geratsdorfer in Weyer, in the district of St. Pantaleon, to be administered for a period of two years by the Agricultural Trust Organization.

Justification: *The real estate is being managed extremely badly by the Geratsdorfer couple and in part is not being managed at all. There are no livestock at all on what is after all a 9 hectare property. The buildings are completely dilapidated.* Admittedly, it may be the case that the lease agreement with the Honorable Mayor Michael Kaltenberger ran out on the first of September, but their property could not be handed back to the owners for the aforesaid reasons. Furthermore, the debts of the couple run to nearly twenty thousand Reichsmarks, and they can not in any way meet their debt liabilities. Witnesses to these facts could of course be cited, namely the Local Leader of the Farmers' Organization in Braunau and Mayor Michael Kaltenberger.

Two hundred and fifty kilometers away, the typewriter of the recording clerk is clattering away officiously in a clinical interrogation room in the Ried Regional Court on the same fourth of September. *The accused is advised to answer the submitted questions precisely, clearly, and in accordance with the truth.* Franz Kubinger clears his throat and begins laboriously to tell the long story of his good idea. In so doing, however, he does not forget to intersperse at regular intervals how innocent he was, how completely innocent. In response to related questions, Franz emphasizes, as if from a prayer wheel, that he, of course, had no inkling at all of violence in the camp.

I have here a letter from the first of July 1940, the Public Prosecutor interrupts. Are you writing in it about weapons and rubber truncheons delivered to the SA sentries? There's no doubt that it was you who wrote that, is there? What purpose should all that stuff have served, in your opinion? Yes, yes, answers Kubinger, all right, all right, but in this document, there's only mention of the delivery, not the utilization. I did not make any decision about that. *That was not part of my brief.* It might perhaps be possible to turn for information to the Major General of the SA Alpenland Branch. Incidentally, when I was there, no prisoner ever complained either. And the injuries, the bandages, didn't you notice them? Yes, certainly, but I was given credible assurances that they were the result of frostbite and wounds acquired in the course of work. And the large numbers away sick, didn't that perplex you? That was the result of abstaining from alcohol, they said. Almost the whole lot were alcoholics, after all. We'll come to that in more detail later, says Dr. Neuwirth.

According to statements from witnesses, you put massive pressure on the regular workers at the Water Authority not to breathe a word about the cases of maltreatment on the building site. Franz Kubinger acts shocked: That must be a misunderstanding. According to my request it was actually inmates' conversations among themselves that were not to be divulged, not any kind of beatings. I wasn't in fact aware of any, as I already pointed out. And your instruction not to make any statements to the Gestapo? There was a particular background to that. *I was informed that Gestapo officials from Salzburg manhandled the Camp Director and wanted to get a confession out of him. In response to that, I said that, if that is the case, then there was something fishy going on. They should not make any statements.* The SA guards in detention awaiting trial unanimously claim that you personally ordered beatings, tying to trees, and similar maltreatment of the so-called racial vermin; even if someone dies in the process, it's all covered, was allegedly your standard response. Is that true? Pack of lies, hisses Franz Kubinger.

Yes, that's good like that, and now a nice smile, look over here! Among Mr. Straffner's portraits in front of the brick wall with its captivating color, there's only one for which the doctor must have got down on his knees: The young girl photographed from below is holding a small child in her arms. Diagonally behind her face is the barbed wire attached to the top of the wall. We see it only in this picture, and it contrasts clearly with her smile, behind that the blue sky, far away.

Names and information about the people who look out at us from these color photographs are for the most part not given, and in any case, it is not possible to assign them to individuals. We know a tiny bit more about those Roma who were already dead when Alois Straffner painstakingly presses the shutter. Therefore, we can't take a picture of them any more – vanished without a trace, all of them, but then again, not quite without a trace. Anyhow, we know, for example, that the camp administration of the Water Authority collects no less than eleven thousand two hundred Reichsmarks in wages for the work regulating the river done by interned Gypsies. For the sake of simplicity, they agree to stipulate a lump sum of one thousand, six hundred marks per month for the whole batch of men employed; complicated individual wage accounting can thus be dispensed with from the outset. When the balance is drawn up for the fiscal year 1941, it's quite clear that this money, without any deductions, is in fact entered in the Reich District of Oberdonau's budget as revenue. There's nobody left alive who could complain about wages withheld. There aren't even proper graves.

For Franz Kubinger, the way he has to proceed is clear. His line of defense for the time being is that his immediate subordinate, Camp Boss August Staudinger, whom he personally appointed, has to play the scapegoat. He's to blame for everything, and Franz accuses him in the presence of the Public Prosecutor. With a bit of luck and a lot of cheek, he can possibly also be framed for the scandalous admissions procedures. At this moment, Staudinger, as a soldier at the Front, is not readily available.

Perhaps, as the Regional Commissioner for Labor Education calculates, a few well-aimed bullets from the enemy will solve the problem in an elegant fashion. From Staudinger, *he never, with the exception of two cases, got any indication that people were being admitted without justification. With respect to the two cases that Staudinger told me about, one was the Hellein case, which I did not know much about, and I cannot recall the second. But no person admitted was released ahead of time because the grounds for admission did not actually tally with the facts.*

Just a moment, Dr. Neuwirth then interrupts Franz; we want to put on record that August Staudinger himself didn't admit anyone; apart from one single known exception; it was you alone. That's correct, but I kept strictly and conscientiously to the applications received and the decrees. And I myself had nothing to do with the group of people to be educated, and therefore complaints didn't come to my attention.

If that's how you see things, Mr. Kubinger, we're forced to go through the cases one at a time. So what happened, for example, in the case of Karl Gumpelmaier? The fact that he refused to buy a Workers' Front flag, that's certainly correct. *But that was not the crucial factor at all. What was significant was that Gumplmayer caused trouble for the firm because of his behavior. I do not know all the details about what exactly Gumplmayer was blamed for. I will only comment, moreover, that in each and every case of an admission concerning a works manager for which I approved the admission on the basis of further instructions from the Gauleiter, I spoke with my superior, the Regional Chairman of the DAF, Party Comrade Stadlbauer. I only sanctioned the admission if Party Member Stadlbauer agreed. If, as I am being accused, the police investigations come to the conclusion that the admission of Gumpelmayer can only be traced back to a personal act of revenge on the part of Gerstl, the DAF District Chairman, then I cannot believe that.*

At this point, we would really like to leave the pitiful

bureaucratic gnome Franz Kubinger alone with the Public Prosecutor; the latter is, after all, paid for listening to such testimony. But Franz is desperate to make us aware of a few more specific details about the fair employment policy in the Third Reich, and we don't want to miss that for anything.

The admission of young people was only authorized by me if the Regional Inspector Schachermayr agreed. I considered Schachermayr to be my superior and therefore undertook to admit the young people, even though, according to the Gauleiter's decree, the admission of young people was not permitted. It is incomprehensible to me how it should turn out according to the investigations that requests for both to be admitted to the Labor Education Camp were only on account of personal differences with Riedler, the Company Youth Counsellor. If I had known the true state of affairs, I would never have admitted the two young people. With reference to the admission of young people, I can only emphasize again that if this admission was sanctioned by myself, it was only ever done after consultation and by order of Schachermayr, the Regional Inspector.

Let's say that the sweat is now in large beads on Franz's forehead. He keeps clearing his throat and requests a glass of water, while the recording clerk tries to bring some sort of order to his sputterings. For months, he has been waiting for a miracle, for the famous *deus ex machina*, which in this political system usually answers to the names of providence and Adolf. Now Regional Unit Leader Senior SA Major Franz Kubinger is certain that his God and the Party, which he's been faithfully serving since 1933, have finally let him down. Here in the Regional Court in Ried in the Inn District, Franz's world is crumbling. While he lets sip by sip slowly run down his throat, he resolves that he will drag all these sons of bitches, all of them, into the abyss with him. The Gauleiter himself knew everything, really and truly everything, he then says for the record, unprompted, and he agreed to everything.

... was sufficient ... because he stayed away from work, that was thus sufficient cause ... I cannot recall ... still stick to the fact that it must be stated in the admission files ... acted as a trouble-maker ... I note that violations of discipline at work, according to the decree of the Reich Trustee ... I even believe that the Reich Trustee insisted that Koller should remain a prisoner.

You have read the minutes of your statements carefully? Is everything presented correctly? Good, then sign here. Yes, you can go now. But please remain available; we will of course inform you in good time about the start of the trial. But I'll probably also need you again in between times to give further information.

Max and Maria Geratsdorfer have a thousand good reasons to object to the unexpected application of the Regional Farmers' Organization: their lawyer makes evidence available to the court according to which the tidy sum of three thousand Reichsmarks was generated in the previous year, even before the leasing. Despite all the difficulties, they delivered the most eggs in the area and the best oats. There are witnesses who can vouch for these claims: the egg dealer and the purchaser of the oats. In the year that just ended, on the other hand, it would of course have been the task of the leaseholder to husband the fields properly. The absence of livestock was also easy to explain: Mayor Kaltenberger had bought the remaining cattle with his own money and was required, according to the contract, to put the same number of animals back in the barn when he surrendered it. The neglect of the buildings was likewise the fault of the leaseholder. Nobody had, however, invested anything, apart from a few doors, in what was henceforth a camp with hundreds of internees.

Furthermore, the debts of the farm owners amounted in reality to only a seventh of the sum that the Director of the Regional Farmers' Organization cites, and they were

Furthermore, the debts of the farm owners amounted in reality to only a seventh of the sum that the Director of the Regional Farmers' Organization cites, and they were also continually being reduced, because in the meantime the farmer had found a temporary job as a bricklayer. Also, there were three children, not just one. At the time, incidentally, the oldest son, Maximilian, was finishing an agricultural apprenticeship with a farmer in St. Pantaleon and had set his heart on taking over the farm later.

Finally, they were at the moment in direct lease negotiations with the District Welfare Organization, which wanted for the time being to continue to run a Gypsy detention camp. They had in fact seen through the fine Mr. Kaltenberger. He not only subleased the estate for half as much again, while all the interest, encumbrances, and taxes continued to be paid by the Geratsdorfers, but the Water Board Authority also additionally paid him a hundred Reichsmarks a month.

It was therefore only too understandable that the mayor could not get over the loss of the sinecure. *He now sets everything in motion to get control of the husbandry of the land again in a roundabout way. Hardly anyone doubts any longer that he himself had initiated the application of the Regional Farmers' Organization of Sept. 4 and that he himself as External Advisor of the Trust Organization wishes to continue to run the business.* To cap it all, after the lease ran out, Kaltenberger illegally prevented Mrs. Geratsdorfer from entering her own land and buildings and also threatened to lock her up. *At the same time, he also berated the woman and called her Gypsy scum. The Geratsdorfer couple struck back most vehemently in face of such tough, ruthless, and exploitative behavior. No German court will be able to lend a helping hand to such proceedings.*

III

Around this time, August Staudinger, escorted by security officers, is sitting with mixed feelings in the train going back to his native Ostmark. The war has developed in an excellent way; the Wehrmacht supreme command is indefatigably announcing victories on all fronts to those who want to listen and to others as well. The military situation seems meanwhile to be appropriate for authorizing the implementation of the arrest warrant for the engineer August Staudinger, which must be further bad tidings for Franz Kubinger. He, meanwhile, is feeling visibly better, and new confidence has taken hold of him.

In October, the Senior Public Prosecutor waits in vain for the accused man. He has issued a summons in good time, but Kubinger does not stir. *In response to a summons sent out with the threat of court proceedings, he communicated by telephone that he was not appearing because the Gauleiter in person had ordered him not to obey the summons.* Dr. Josef Neuwirth smells a rat because an important witness in the forthcoming proceedings, the District Commissioner of the German Labor Front in Linz, likewise allows the date of the hearing to creep past without giving a reason.

The proceedings of the Regional Farmers' Organization against the Geratsdorfer couple in the Agricultural Court in Wildshut also drag on. In this case, Gauleiter August Eigruber would prefer for understandable reasons to be lucky sooner rather than later. He, therefore, under the awesome letterhead "The Reich Governor of Oberdonau, Regional Self-Administration," gives the small provincial judge a few useful tips to guide him to a decision. As boss of the District Welfare Organization, Eigruber would naturally only be prepared to enter into a lease agreement with the Geratsdorfers *if the directive for trustees to manage the estate which I* wholeheartedly supported *were rejected*. Extremely concerned about the present uncovenanted state of the Gypsy Detention Camp, the Gauleiter asks the court to reach a decision as soon as possible.

Indeed, as far as the judiciary is concerned, Eigruber will have to sort out everything for himself. As is right and proper, the Attorney General does not want NSDAP verdicts to take legal effect simply and automatically. Thus, the Gauleiter, for example, gets to hear in this early autumn of 1941 that Dr. Köllinger had been impudent enough to initiate further inquiries with reference to the pillorying of one Mrs. Böhm from Linz, who was consorting with a Czech. But for both Franz Kubinger and August Eigruber, sexual outrage against the German nation is a matter for the boss and without exception to be relentlessly avenged: *in order to simplify the necessary extensive inquiries in wartime, when there is a lack of manpower anyway, I am informing you that I myself ordered the pillorying, and that all those involved acted on my instructions. If you need any further information at all, please turn exclusively to me.*

Heil Hitler!

In other parts of the Reich, a relatively large number of Roma and Sinti are still at large. For a time compulsory sterilizations seem to be the approved means of getting a grip on what the Nazi mentality considered to be the nauseating propagation of this asocial tribe. What wins medals and state eulogies for German mothers in St. Pantaleon, namely bringing as many offspring into the world as possible, is considered in the case of the Gypsies to be striking proof of sexual dissoluteness and racial inferiority. From one day to the next, the official registers must contain legally binding abbreviations like Z, ZM. ZM I gr., ZM II gr. to indicate Gypsies (*Zigeuner*) and Gypsy half-castes (ZM) of various degrees (gr.).

For the gypsies interned in Weyer, these bureaucratic innovations are, in reality, of hardly any significance. Right from the very start, the efficiency of the Romanies on the building site was not particularly satisfactory. They bore no comparison with the earlier prisoners because God knows those really worked hard; nobody can deny that. But something like that was of course to be expected; right from the very start, the Water Authority thought the business of the Gypsy Camp was a crazy idea. Rabble which has never learned to work is just not going to accomplish anything decent, no matter how strict the supervision. It's really a pity that the cornered Party Members had to spirit away all the able-bodied workers from the camp on the spur of the moment just because of a crazy gang of SA thugs. They really had no choice.

As far as the outside world was concerned, everything of course had to look as if it had been planned for a long while, and that's why they naturally had to let the grass grow over the affair for some time. All right, that's somehow understandable. Realistically, the Gypsies should have been sent packing right away after a week, but what sort of message would that have sent? For every man halfway fit for work in the camp, there's a woman and at least two offspring; you just have to imagine what that's like. Fucking, they're almost as good at that as at stealing, and they breed like rabbits. In the long term, let's be honest, we all have to fork out for swanky holiday quarters for this work-shy, parasitic rabble, keeping them safe in the outback, while our own sons are out there on the battlefield suffering dreadful deprivation and dying for their country. A business relying on subsidies, a bottomless barrel is what this camp is. Can we really afford a sanatorium like that in the middle of the war?

It's not only at the regulars' table in the village pub that people are passionately weighing costs and benefits. The future of the whole enterprise at Waidmoos is ultimately ill fated. It's time to beat an orderly retreat. In August, on instructions from above, the Roma cease their work on the river regulation project. Moreover, from September onwards, when the lease runs out, the camp hovers in a situation not covered by the law. Meanwhile, it is to be anticipated that these exasperating proceedings will go on for months. Witnesses must be summoned, further statements must be obtained, and it cannot even be ruled out that in a roundabout way sleeping dogs may be wakened. What if, for example, the condition of the buildings is inspected by experts? What if they come around unannounced and see what's going on?

First of all, other senior officials come along. Under the leadership of the Reich Moorland Advisor Dr. Baden from Berlin, a large conference on moor management is taking place in St. Pantaleon. In order to take the wind out of the sails of the growing number of those skeptical about the advisability of the crisis-shaken mammoth project, one last concerted effort is being made, albeit of a purely theoretical nature. This is an opportunity for impressive scientific support for an ideological stance with which people have been familiar for ages: We're actually creating living space in abundance for you. *The moor is also covered in places with a layer of 10 to 20 centimeters of minerals. Whereas moorland in general primarily provides high-quality grassland, moorland with a moderate covering of minerals also guarantees permanently arable land. Business management investigations will create the prerequisite for an efficient distribution of the newly developed farmland among the owners who at present have a share of the moorland.*

The controversial drainage project is desperately in need of a positive image and new impetus. It will therefore also soon be necessary as a concomitant measure to spirit away the Gypsies, together with their wives and children. But by what means? It then comes like a gift of providence that people in higher places are soon intending to dispatch five thousand Gypsies from Styria and Burgenland to Litzmannstadt to occupy a new ghetto that's being established in a place where it's guaranteed that they won't be a burden on anyone's pocket for long. Lodz was once the Polish name of this metropolis, which, with its 750,000 inhabitants, according to the latest radio communications, is now the sixth largest city in the German Reich. If we could just send them there, the Gordian knot could be cut painlessly, they say exultantly in the Gauleiter's office in Linz and hope for sympathy from their Party Comrades in Burgenland.

Fair enough, if the Oberdonau people are absolutely set on it, let's just pack up the seven hundred Gypsies here in Lackenbach. With our three hundred, we'll have the planned number of one thousand. Yes, please guarantee to send them down to us by the fourth of November; we're really only reloading them; then it's on immediately from there, together with the trains from Hartberg and Fürstenfeld and from Oberwart and Rotenturm on the Pinka river, exactly a thousand per train, so five thousand in total, at the very most thirty kilos of luggage per head or per nose.

During these weeks, it's not only the moor management conference and its prestigious participants that give a massive propaganda boost to the river regulation project that's come to a standstill but also the regional newspaper. With reference to the story told up to now and the imminent and highly efficient mass murder of those who up to then had been compulsory workers along with their families, we also come to a momentary standstill ourselves, despite all we know, when we read in black and white: *therefore, despite the war, a great peace initiative is being born in Ibm-Waidmoos, the creation of new land to cultivate, new land to farm in the midst of soil where old German peasants have settled.* The proud author, by the way, signs himself M.K., and somehow or other these initials seem familiar to us.

For the last time, on the morning of October 18 in Weyer camp, a child is born. The camp administrators recognized as early as May that calling in a midwife was an excessive indulgence and put an end to the nonsense. You see, the birth can take place without one: It's a girl. Her mother, Juliana Held, gives her the name of Marie. Yes, Held [hero], of all things, is indeed the name of mother and child, a word whose use in the Third Reich is becoming frequent and is usually combined with death. And that's what mother and daughter Held have to face just a few weeks later. Michael Kaltenberger signs the birth certificate in routine fashion, and we presume that at this point he has long since known what is planned for the exactly three hundred remaining Roma. Sorry, with Marie Held that makes three hundred and one.

A file note made on the first of November in the Linz Attorney General's Office records that discussions took place between the Reich Ministry of Justice and the Party Headquarters concerning the case of Franz Kubinger. Therefore, in order to bring the charges against the GLF Regional Unit Leader and Administrator of Labor Education, procedural caution had to be recommended to the Senior Public Prosecutor. Dr. Neuwirth is therefore urgently advised to modify his original draft dramatically if he really wishes to hold Kubinger to account. In particular, he should dispense with the charges of offenses that might bring leading NSDAP functionaries to the witness box or even to the dock. The best thing, of course, once things developed, would be not to separate the proceedings against Franz Kubinger after all and to bring in an additional charge against him in the main proceedings against August Staudinger and others. In a word: the political dimension of the case must be eliminated; otherwise, all the effort would probably be in vain. In any case, there was enough evidence to put Kubinger behind bars for years.

Early tomorrow morning, trucks will come and pick you up, is what's suddenly announced behind the Weyer camp walls. You're allowed to take one bag full of possessions with you; valuables are to be left behind. Because there's so much snow, we'll even save you the walk to the station; aren't we nice? By the way, in case you're curious, you're off to beautiful Burgenland, if you know where that is. It's where you won't be so much on your own any more, where there are already many other Gypsies; where there's a huge settlement just for people like yourselves, a present from the Führer.

Many inmates, especially children, have no shoes, and therefore haven't emerged from their housing for weeks. They cry and scream, then are silent and only open their eyes wide when they are herded barefoot over the early snow to the truck. So it is quite still, snowy-still on the site. What remains are armies of fleas, the subject of much further talk in the village, because the insects have to look for new places to live and will attach themselves to the people who'll be cleaning the camp.

In Bürmoos station, sufficient freight cars are waiting on a siding. The German State Railroad has long since assigned large steam engines to the local line with its once idyllically short little trains. Peat extraction, brick production, and lumbering are now in full swing; a huge supraregional repair center for traction vehicle engines is being planned. So transports like this one hardly attract any attention, and it's especially the railwaymen themselves, many of whom belong to the active resistance movement, who have a lasting memory of them. They're quite surprised that it's not the SA or the SS giving the orders but the police.

Hurry up, hurry up, get a move on, get a move on. Hurry up at the back. Don't fall asleep, ladies and gentlemen. Two hundred and ninety-eight, two hundred and ninety-nine, three hundred, three hundred and one. Done. The last wagon is secured according to the regulations; the starting signal sounds; the train slowly sets off. And while we gaze after it as it throws up swirls of snow, takes the wide left-hand curve, and whistles loudly before it disappears in the forest and only the plume of smoke high above the trees betrays its accelerated speed, we anticipate in telegram style what will happen to the passengers. They're actually little more than freight.

For three days, they'll swell the numbers of those occupying the Gypsy Detention Camp in Lackenbach to one thousand, six hundred and twenty-nine, and then on the seventh of November, they'll depart for Litzmannstadt according to plan. That's where four thousand, nine hundred and ninety-six living and eleven dead Gypsies are unloaded. The Gypsy ghetto, prepared in great haste and angrily rejected from the outset by the local Commandants, is a whole two hundred meters long and barely sixty meters wide. The blocks of houses between Towianska Street, Starosikawska Street, and Glowacka Street are separated from their huge Jewish counterparts (huge in terms of the numbers of people herded together there but likewise still also ridiculously small) by a double barbed-wire fence and a filled-in moat. The windows to the outside world on Brzezinska Street, now called Sulzfelder Street, are boarded and nailed up. Almost every building has several balconies on each floor, with a view over the barbed wire. They, of course, are just as barricaded as the windows. Furniture is next to non-existent in the city houses abandoned by their Polish inhabitants. So those incarcerated have to sleep on the floor; there's hardly anything to eat and no fuel. The oldest of the one hundred and fifty-seven thousand Jews interned in Lodz are instructed to share the much too scarce food rations with the Gypsies. Medicines and doctors are not assigned, with the exception of certain Jewish medics from across the way, brought there by fate. For all five thousand Romanies, the stated cause of death – for the sake of simplicity and because in any case nobody will question it – is cardiac weakness. In reality they're dying, the children fastest of all, of cold, starvation, and debilitation; in the first week alone, there are no fewer than two hundred and thirteen corpses. But most contract typhus fever, which, because of the disastrous sanitary conditions, breaks out as early as November and wreaks terrible havoc. The hearses, which, according to the duty roster, should not be underway until after nine in the morning, are soon going regularly as early as six into the so-called Gypsy reservation. Laid out with wise foresight, the new Jewish cemetery at the edge of the ghetto has generous proportions. A special area in it is marked off, and the Romanies are hastily buried there. Their death rate exceeds that of the Jews from across the way by one hundred percent. But writing that down almost sounds cynical. Any Gypsy who has the insolence to manage to survive the turn of the year 1941-42 is shipped off as a punishment to Kulmhof (Chelmno) fifty-five kilometers away. There are special experimental vehicles there for toxic gas treatment. The corpses produced in them are buried for the first few days in a nearby forest until a specially constructed incineration plant is installed next to the camouflaged buses. Now the mass graves are also opened again and their contents burned; a bone crusher grinds up the most intractable remains. On the twelfth of January these Gypsies are completely and without exception eliminated, and in Kulmhof the Jews are now being attended to.

In the meantime, a smart red- and ivory-colored passenger train with steamed-up windows has arrived in Bürmoos from the opposite direction. Anyone who gets too lost in his own thoughts forgets completely that the world continues to revolve. Two elderly women in kerchiefs climb ponderously out of the modern, gasoline-driven, local train, which will be completely destroyed in exactly three years in an allied bomb attack on the way back to the depot in Salzburg. A man with a briefcase and a wide-brimmed hat climbs out, full of verve; the friendly conductor helps a young mother with two children out of the coach. We think it's a doll the girl is clutching tightly, and hardly has the lad touched ground before he's high-spiritedly making a snowball. The platform's sanded according to the regulations.

The world continues, as we said, to revolve, and while three hundred and one people from St. Pantaleon are reloaded in Lackenbach on the sixth of November 1941, the District Farmers' Community in Braunau leaps passionately into the breach for the mayor regarding the matter of the Weyer farm estate. Michael Kaltenberger may admittedly have sold the cattle belonging to the Geratsdorfer couple, but he immediately handed over the proceeds to them in cash. A replacement in kind was never envisaged. Furthermore, one horse was in such bad shape that it was only fit for emergency slaughter.

After these first heartening measures against the Gypsy Plague, Gauleiter and Reich Governor August Eigruber now wants to make sure that the embarrassing matter of the Labor Education Camp he inherited is lifted. In the middle of November, he arranges for the correct names of all the accused to be forwarded, as well as the appropriate reference numbers from the Public Prosecutor's Office and the Ministry. He addresses a formal request for cancellation to the Reich Ministry of Justice. It arrives in Berlin shortly before Christmas, pretty much at the same time as the Public Prosecutor's final draft of the indictment.

Dr. Josef Neuwirth has taken to heart the proposals of his superior: he now sees himself obliged under these circumstances to indict the perpetrator, bureaucrat Franz Kubinger after all, together with his fellow practitioners, his SA comrades. He intends to leave aside the points regarding misuse of authority and incitement to criminal action. *Furthermore, for the prosecution of Franz Kubinger on account of unjustified admissions, it would be necessary to question as witnesses the Gauleiter and Reich Governor of Oberdonau about the legal accuracy of Kubinger's liability, with a view to its possible refutation. But in order to do this, consent would first have to be obtained because of the law concerning the questioning of members of the NSDAP decreed on December 1, 1936, Reich Law Gazette, I.S.994.* But the Public Prosecutor no longer dares to do that. He's had to take into account, whether he likes it or not, that Party Members are above the law once they've risen to a certain rank on the functionaries' ladder.

The procedures in the Litzmannstadt ghetto (the official term is now "resettlement") are a socially fitting prelude to the final solution. In Berlin, the Nazi elite are gathering for the legendary Wannsee Conference. The Third Reich is taking action; from now on, they'll be doing things properly. It would take legions of upright Public Prosecutors to resist, as Dr. Neuwirth did, the brown tide, making public the names and fates of individual victims and bombarding the Reich Ministry of Justice with bills of indictment, meticulously researched, of course.

Meanwhile, the forlorn grounds of the Weyer camp appear completely deserted. It is not until the end of February 1942 that the trial is held at the Agricultural Court. From the outset, the farmers are fighting a losing battle; all their well-founded objections are simply swept off the table. As a witness, Mayor Michael Kaltenberger tells a pack of lies. In order to provide evidence of that, we sit down inconspicuously behind the assessors with the newly published 1941 balance of accounts for the Reich District of Oberdonau's budget and go through it again carefully.

I committed myself to pay a rent of 100 Reichsmarks per month to the Geratsdorfer couple and did not myself receive more than 100 Reichsmarks for the subleasing. I therefore did not make a profit from this lease contract and only attended to the matter in the "public interest," is what Michael Kaltenberger proudly states, as usual without blushing. We consult the tables of our hefty volume and read in the budget subsection Nr. 19 for the Gypsy Detention Camp in Weyer, St. Pantaleon, under Item 16 in the expenditure column, a) Ongoing expenses, 2. Material expenses: *Rent for the house, 1200 Reichsmarks.* Moreover, the comments column advises us on the same line: *8 months* – meaning January until the end of the lease in August – *at 150 Marks.* It is extremely improbable that the astute Honorable District Party Group Leader raked in less for the first camp and leased the Geratsdorfers' fields to someone else for free. And he has nothing whatsoever to say about what the indictment maintains are direct allocations from the Water Authority.

Further examples of Kaltenberger's creative handling of the truth could be appended, for example the callously alleged generous investments of District Welfare funds into the maintenance of the buildings, but the court is not giving us any time. This is because the two older children of the farmers have just been summoned. The parents have maintained that all three were prepared to help them later in running the farm, not that we may now expect that the judge will consult the young people in detail about it. In fact, they're *given a close interrogation. Franziska, although already over 20 years of age, is a small, sickly creature with a delicate voice and delicate hands and does not give the impression of being a farmer's child. She is dressed in city clothes and also has city manners. If anything, Max has more the appearance of a farmer's child. But he is still very childish in nature.*

Well, if that's the case, we can move straight to the verdict: In the name of the German nation! Thanks to the statement of witness Michael Kaltenberger, there *seems to be a sufficiency of evidence that the Geratsdorfer couple were never successful in keeping their farm in even halfway satisfactory condition and so on. Max and Maria Geratsdorfer, the people entitled to work it, are obliged to pay the costs of the proceedings.* On the surface, it appears that the Agricultural Trust Association may thus look forward to a new property to manage. But what's really to be done with it, now that its last inhabitants have long since been gassed or died of typhoid and starvation?

A new use is being considered. The bottom line is that the operational deficit for 1941 comes officially to eighty-two thousand Reichsmarks. This is a disaster. In any case, people in the area are sick of the presence of asocials, Gypsies, and other rabble. For a time, a smart Hitler Youth Farm Service Camp is seriously considered but never opened. Consequently, it will be early 1944 before seminars in preventive pharmacy can be held in the buildings at the order of the Reich Commissioner for Defense for the Reich Defense Region of Oberdonau. After two years have elapsed, the Trust Management no longer wishes to take on time-consuming projects; after all, it's only a matter of time until the phrase "Home Front" unexpectedly gains real significance. The grounds are simply impounded for the duration of the war.

The sheds and stables, by the way, have to serve as

housing for irreplaceable equipment like X-ray and diathermy machines, microscopes, field laboratories, and the like. It is doubtless regrettable that the Geratsdorfers' agricultural machines have therefore to be parked in the open air. They object, admittedly more timidly than before, but nothing can be done about it.

We've once again gotten ahead of ourselves. It is hardly surprising that in the Ministry of Justice in Berlin in 1942 there are worries more serious than these exasperating, provincial Ostmark camp antics. The indictments remain unfinished business, but there are also no signs whatsoever that the proceedings may be dismissed. Josef Mayrlehner and Alois Rosenbichler have been in detention more than a year awaiting trial; some time ago, August Staudinger joined them. Senior Public Prosecutor Neuwirth is gradually becoming impatient, Gauleiter Eigruber angry. At the beginning of March, he once again calls the Attorney General to his office. Meanwhile, the latter is used to it. No, he doesn't have any new information from the Ministry, says Dr. Köllinger regretfully. The Gauleiter again offers the transparent suggestion that the accused be set free again for the time being. Dr. Köllinger remains resolute. *In response to my objection that, given the present state of the criminal proceedings, there can be no question of the three accused men being released from prison before sentence is passed, he asks me to present his request for release to the Reich Minister for Justice. I agree to this.* What else can he possibly do?

On that very same day, the Attorney General writes to Berlin to this effect. In so doing, he leaves no shadow of doubt that he considers political interventions in such serious criminal cases to be unreasonable. Nevertheless, two weeks later, Gauleiter Eigruber seems to have achieved his aim. He contacts Dr. Köllinger by phone and says triumphantly that he has a telegram direct from the

Führer's Chancellery in front of him on his desk. The Führer has cancelled the proceedings against Alois Rosenbichler and comrades. Their immediate discharge is anticipated.

At that moment, Dr. Köllinger's door in Linz is already opening, and Mr. Belzeder from Ried in the Inn District asks to be permitted to sit down. Belzeder is at the moment in charge of the Public Prosecutor's Office there and reports with some concern that it is some days since the District authorities in Ried were apparently informed direct from Berlin that the Weyer camp issue will not end up in court. The Regional Court is thus under massive pressure. The colleague makes it clear to Dr. Köllinger that the aggravated situation with his superior is making people very jumpy. What's to be done?

In response, Dr. Anton Köllinger first adds a further comment to the file under the finicky reference number 405E – R 8/40. To give him due credit: even in this extremely difficult situation – the game which was serious for him and now seems to be as good as lost – he still has enough guts to use the word "allegedly" in the written submission when he makes a note of various telegrams and telephone calls between the individual offices of the NSDAP concerning the cancellation of the proceedings. Of course, Köllinger finally instructs the visibly relieved Public Prosecutor Belzeder to release the prisoners held for questioning without delay. But he'd actually like to have it in writing.

The Gauleiter is evidently not able to help him. Obviously, there's something brewing, and it may be that no less a man than Adolf Hitler himself has mumbled crossly into the phone that the tiresome matter is to be settled immediately; you'll get the paperwork on your desk this very day. August Eigruber's eager request will obviously have given rise to these thoughts, and it may well be (on the basis of previous experience) that he has every confidence that the bluff that was argued so confidently and reinforced by brandishing a make-believe telegram in front of the telephone receiver will fool the Oberdonau judiciary. The fact remains that, although officially the case is neither altered nor terminated, the incarcerated accused will be set free immediately. For almost one and a half years now, the judiciary has been resisting effectively, but let's not fool ourselves – the resistance is near to caving in.

Even in the third year of the war, spring begins punctually on the twenty-first of March. But that's of secondary importance. Because on the twenty-first of March 1942, Fritz Sauckel is appointed Plenipotentiary-General for Labor Mobilization. At the same time, substantial areas of the Department of Employment are put under his control. In the occupied regions, Sauckel has so-called recruiting commissions set up, and from now on, the war economy of the Nazi state will rely substantially on the systematic exploitation of forced labor and on foreign workers. Little Franz Kubinger, that miserable failure of a Regional Commissioner for Labor Education in Oberdonau, has to go pale with envy when he thinks about the mighty terms of reference of the great Fritz Sauckel. Furthermore, the Sword of Damocles continues to hang over him: will there finally be a trial after all, despite all the assurances of the Regional Administration?

At this point, it is announced throughout the whole Reich that meat, fat, bread, and sugar will be drastically rationed, beginning April 1. Michael Kaltenberger has the exceedingly unpleasant task at the end of March, under Item two of the order of business, of sending out the appropriate instructions to his District Council. Immediately after an emotional tribute to recently fallen heroes from the village, the mayor gives *the Council members instructions to suppress any possible differences of opinions by keeping these people constantly aware of the necessity of these measures.* In the confidential reports of the Security Service of the SS, there is talk of the fact that the announcements may have had a more devastating effect on the population than almost any other event during the war so far.

"Confidential" is also written on a document of much less significance for the general public, which bears the date of April 16, 1942: *With the authorization of the Führer I dismiss the criminal proceedings against 1.) the butcher August Staudinger, 2.) the laborer Alois Rosenbichler, 3.) the carpenter's assistant Josef Mayrlehner, 4.) the Camp Director Josef Wieger, 5.) the Regional Unit Leader Franz Kubinger. Signed by The Reich Minister for Justice.* Oh yes, and: *I request that the accused, Alois Rosenbichler, Josef Mayrlehner, and August Staudinger, be released from custody immediately.* Of course, that has already happened. So now, even though it's outrageous, it's actually official. The files on the case of the Labor Education Camp in Weyer, district of St. Pantaleon, are closed this twenty-fourth of April.

It remains to add that the Honorable Public Prosecutors may now have lost any chance of influencing the course of events. But all the same, they can see that all the files, originals, and copies remain intact and are carefully filed. They still place a vague hope in later generations and, according to their political position, hope for a future Nazi state structure after the war, whatever it may be like, which has a certain scope for development and a more powerful judiciary that's not directly controlled by the Party. They may even hope for a real constitutional state, which admittedly seems to be light years away.

In Linz and Ried, as indeed throughout the whole of the Third Reich, many politically motivated and shameful verdicts have long since been issued, even if only existing laws are implemented, as the respectable gentlemen in their worthy robes legitimate themselves some years later. Under this regime, executions are carried out as if on an assembly line, and the newspapers list in every edition who is to be punished by death and why. We admit shamefacedly that we didn't accompany our Public Prosecutors to other trials, whether it was because we simply didn't have the time or because we were frightened that our respect for their upright progress in the Weyer affair could under certain circumstances be significantly affected. We do not know more about them than we are relating and therefore ask for the reader's understanding.

By the way, after his release, Alois Rosenbichler immediately assumes a new post as an unscathed man. He continues to make himself useful as a medical orderly in the nearby Ranshofen aluminum works.

IV

Three full years later. A man rushes into the district offices. The Americans have already got almost as far as Braunau, he blurts out breathlessly, as if he'd just covered the whole long distance on foot. Gnashing his teeth, Mayor Michael Kaltenberger refrains from shooting the defeatist on the spot. Instead, the great District Party Group Leader will be busy in the coming days burning great bundles of files from the time between 1938 and 1945. He develops admirable staying power and thoroughness; only a very few documents escape his rampage of elimination. Nobody in the village has the courage to stop him, and many also lack the interest.

Kaltenberger suspects that one of the next days will be his last in office. He's only forty-five, so he's making comprehensive provision for the time to come. Many a village inhabitant does in fact have a score or two to settle with him. A few weeks in prison on the personal recommendation of the mayor as punishment for consorting with French prisoners of war could, for example, make a certain farmer bear a grudge; people like the Geratsdorfer family will now be rising in the world and, out of pure vindictiveness, will argue that in reality he never had good intentions towards them. The clerics will probably also not show him Christian forgiveness for all the regrettable misunderstandings, and it's not out of the question that the forced laborers from a wide range of nationalities have a bone they want to pick with him before they return to their homelands. Little Alexander, for example, religion: Orthodox, born illegitimately in St.

Pantaleon, hometown: Kursk, is not yet under the ground. He's the first one since the Gypsy child Rudolf Haas four years ago whose cause of death is officially specified by Dr. Straffner as a fatal debility. Ten days later, Alexander's mother, a Russian farmgirl and forced laborer, will have survived serfdom; the war is finally over. A rabid Ukrainian will take this as grounds to shoot down in his office the Nazi mayor of the neighboring village of St. Georgen. It's painful to think about former inmates of the camp knocking at Kaltenberger's front door in the coming months, about the victor's judiciary again initiating the trial that he's just escaped by a hair's breadth.

He has two glimmers of hope left. One of them is the merrily flickering fire in front of him that he's patiently feeding with new sustenance in the form of documents from the shelves of the district administration. The other one is the millions of people who died in the death camps, the millions of dead people on the battlefields, Europe in rubble and ashes. Given all of that, they'll probably let small fry like him slip through the net, he persuades himself: the few dead people in Weyer would be of no consequence given the outrageously bloody events in this mighty struggle of the nations.

At all events, on the third of May, there is indeed no Mayor Kaltenberger any more, and the next day Gauleiter August Eigruber, together with his best friend Stefan Schachermayr from Linz, escapes to Kirchdorf on the Krems, from where he, for one last time, broadcasts stiff-upper-lip slogans over the radio. Both gentlemen will strengthen their man-to-man friendship in an idyllic mountain hut over the next few months and hope at some point in the future to be able to escape to foreign lands unrecognized. In the middle of August, people purporting to help them flee do, it's true, provide a car for them, but also provide an effective roadblock around a blind bend.

The two heroes are taken by surprise and arrested without any appreciable resistance.

The St. Pantaleon theater company has been in existence since 1910. *The Second World War, however, forced it to take a compulsory break. In order to distract the politically activated spirits in the village, Mayor Anton Veichtlbauer recommended in 1945 that plays be produced again.* We learn this from the municipal chronicle that appeared decades later, published by the district. Apart from two short notices about the League of Comradeship and the Organization for War Victims, the time between 1938 and 1945 hardly appears in it at all. It seems that there were never camps here, and because of the draining of the moor, the mills on the Moosach were deprived of their source of power, reads the one and only sentence which could bring us closer to other exhausted sources of power, if it wanted.

According to newspaper reports, some of those citizens of pre-1938 Germany proved to be downright ungrateful after being evacuated from the bombed ruins of their cities and often enjoying the hospitality of Austrians in the Innviertel for years. House facades in St. Pantaleon decorated in the dead of night by graffiti artists remain behind as souvenirs when these fine gentlemen are deported to their home country. You can see the words, for example: *Farewell, you stupid Österreich [Austria], we're going home to our own Reich!*

The farsighted plan of the new mayor to distract the overwrought political spirits by working together on Ludwig Ganghofer's popular drama *The Crucifix Sculptor of Oberammergau* threatens for a time to miscarry because many in the village simply don't want to be distracted. On the contrary, they perceive it as a provocation that a few months after the end of the Hitler era people who were just a short time ago entrenched Nazis should be playing roles in a play like that, as if nothing had happened. For the time being, the rehearsals have to be postponed, and only with difficulty do they nevertheless succeed, in the face of substantial opposition, in obtaining a license to perform from the District Authority in Braunau. The brilliant success of the production will, however, soon open the critics' eyes to the fact that it's ultimately pointless to try to swim against the tide.

The denazification is already in full swing. With the *Forms for Registration of National Socialists* in front of them, many former members get into a real sweat. For example, Karl Hiebler, Hans Mells, and Dr. Alois Straffner, once Council members, at first sought *Exemption from Registration*. It didn't help at all. At the start of 1946, when it gets serious, the memories of the many people forced to supply information are already very selective. Straffner no longer recalls that he served the Party in his post as District Department Manager of the National Socialist People's Welfare and was regularly collecting more or less voluntary donations to it from the population; Hiebler's statements are so false that he seems confused about his identity. He was neither a functionary nor an ordinary member of the National Socialist Motor Transport Corps, he believes, and he didn't join the party until the autumn of 1938. He claims to have resigned as early as 1942, again over a dispute. We do still have a lively recollection of Hiebler's NSKK speeches, which were also praised in the newspaper. A resentful St. Pantaleon citizen promptly lodges an objection with the district, saying she knows for a fact that Karl had been an illegal member of the Nazi Party since 1932 and a fanatical Nazi propagandist.

That's also how the District Court in Ried sees things when it confirms that since 1932 Mr. Karl Hiebler had been the proud owner of the low Nazi Party membership number 121405. Over and above that, there is the following personal entry in his NS personal file from 1938: *dedicated myself publicly at all times to the NSDAP and publicly declared my commitment to the movement everywhere.* Mr. Hiebler, NS District Propaganda Leader for St. Pantaleon, emphasized at that time, among other things, the fact that in the now historical Austria he had, for political reasons, been convicted for *insulting the honor of a Jew (expression used: bloody Jew).* These preserved documents are a bitter setback, but soon the man will rise again like a phoenix from the ashes. Ex-NSDAP Organization Leader Hans Mells will in the end satisfactorily manage the large Salzburg brewery for twenty more years. The new district representatives evidently want to exonerate him but use an extremely idiosyncratic logic when they ask people to bear in mind that: *his National Socialist disposition was well known, but not remarkable, since he is a Reich German.*

Meanwhile, Gottfried Haimbuchner, August Staudinger, and Josef Wieger are about to be admitted to the Marcus W. Orr Camp in Glasenbach near Salzburg where other troubled National Socialists like Michael Kaltenberger have for some time been gloomily awaiting the things that are about to happen. Alois Rosenbichler is declared missing in Austria but has managed within a short period to rise to become business manager of a painting firm in Germany that lacked a boss after the war. The female partner is extremely pleased with him. His old colleague Josef Mayrlehner is found dead under mysterious circumstances on January 31, 1946, near Katsdorf in the Mühlviertel region. That is fine for some, since much can then conveniently be blamed on the dead man in the coming People's Court trials.

In the confusion of the past year, the *New Watch on the Inn* has had to cease appearing for a few months. Now it's back again, and although paper is still scarce, there's already space for a few rather lengthy articles, such as the one in this edition penned by Ludwig Weinberger. "Nature Conservation and the Ibmer Moor" is its title. The man argues competently and pointedly for the preservation of a piece of valuable primeval landscape. We discover that it had been a financial object of interest for many years, and that there are still persons for whom ideals have no value, where their only concern is the economy. Weinberger initially recalls the first attempt at drainage in the year 1935, an attempt which was a pitiful failure, as is generally known. There is no shortage of well-founded criticisms of the NSDAP's megalomaniac plans to drain the area, and the author conveys graphically to us what things looked like at that time on the former building site, which, despite all the ambitious announcements, was abandoned with little discussion shortly after the closing of the camp. All of two kilometers were completed. *Soon the dimensions of the canal become smaller; it starts to leak, then there are areas that have collapsed, sloppy structural work, and finally a section in which the Gypsies were grubbing around. Yet again the construction work remained stuck in the dirt.*

This is in fact probably the first time after the war that the Weyer Romanies are mentioned at all in the records, as an afterthought, of course, without wasting a single word on why they were grubbing around in the moorland and what became of them. Perhaps it's our fault if we hear their fleas from that period still coughing, if we suspect that the dedicated environmental pioneer might, for hygienic reasons, have done better not to let a few hundred out of a half a million recently murdered Roma and Sinti "grub around" so intrusively between the words "leak," "sloppy," and "dirt."

But it will be fifty years until the linguistic dictatorship of the regime will be recognized as a public nuisance; for the time, the realities are being communicated, mostly uncontradicted, between the lines, even if people are no longer allowed to speak as clearly about certain things as they were a year ago. Where they, the Nazis, are to be criticized, they must, however, be mercilessly criticized, thanks to the restored freedom of the press. For example, they really weren't great nature conservationists.

Two months later, on April 1, 1946, Haigermoos takes its leave again of St. Pantaleon. The village gains back the independence which it lost eight years before, and we would like to rejoice about it with the people of Haigermoos. The matter has only one little snag: from now on, nobody will need to feel responsible for the camp in Weyer because it didn't exist at all then as a district, as people in Haigermoos will argue with some degree of justification. Weyer? That's actually outside our district boundaries, we no longer have anything to do with it, will be what, on the other hand, people in St. Pantaleon will say. The corpses distributed over the two cemeteries may spell out a clear message, but nobody wants to hear it. And for the resurrected federal state of Upper Austria, the former regional camp for the whole of Oberdonau is one hundred and fifty kilometers too far away from Linz to be visible at all in these postwar years. What do we seriously want to say in response to the observation that on average probably almost as many prisoners perished in Mauthausen every day in 1940/41 as in the two Weyer camps in total? Before everything can be thoroughly repressed, we only need the trials. Unfortunately, there'll be no escaping them.

In Glasenbach camp, a good thirty kilometers away from St. Pantaleon, the days pass uniformly and pretty drearily for the former Weyer guards. The American military authorities dispense completely with the labor force of internees, which means that the latter have a great deal of free time. Admittedly, the ex-mayor and our three ex-SA leaders officially receive food which is as scarce and as poor in quality as their education victims formerly received, but relatives and friends are at liberty to send them food parcels. Anyone who doesn't get anything from home is mostly fed something out of solidarity among the inmates; it's a well-known fact that in these circles the public good comes before self-interest.

Unless, that is, someone speaks up and responds, for example, to the gripping in-house lecture in the camp about Admiral Dönitz's last pathetic words before the capitulation. There is talk of reverential bowing down in front of fallen comrades, obligation to silent obedience and so on – with the sarcastic comment *"Helmets off! Time to pray!"* and a bitter laugh. One person *grabs that scoundrel by the jacket collar and pushes him* into the corridor where he beats him. *He was an upright man who did not make a big fuss but immediately took action. He did not let the defiling of dead comrades go unpunished, and when injustice occurred, he did not edge bashfully to one side and keep silent; he went for it.*

This is the vigorous tone in which some revealing memoirs of Glasenbach people are written. As early as 1950, they are noticeably livening up the Austrian book market and mostly running through several editions. Attacks by young US guard soldiers on isolated individuals within crowds of more than ten thousand internees are exaggerated and described by most of these authors as acts of terror. Documentary films about the liberated concentration camps are ridiculed as poorly made, and black guards or any of Mexican origin are described gleefully with unconcealed racism, just as was the widespread custom in the United States at this time.

Many of those erroneously arrested must doubtless vegetate here for months, for example, before they manage to prove a simple mistaken identity. For countless guilt-ridden inmates, such examples are, admittedly, reason enough to classify themselves in the ranks of victims of the victors' judiciary, without a scrap of self-criticism and shame. August, Gottfried, Josef, and Michael may not indeed have written any books, but they will complain bitterly to their wives and friends about the hard life in the camp. It is beyond a doubt that they, like many comrades who shared the same fate, see themselves only as political prisoners.

In Glasenbach, countless Nazi intellectuals, artists, and generals sit alongside normal mortals. They soon provide a wide range of educational opportunities that make the time go faster, raise morale, and are therefore very popular. Often several lectures and cultural events take place on the same day. A former senior commander, for example, gives a two-hour lecture on the first part of his observations on the "Dispatch and Return of the Lapland Army to Norway in the Arctic Winter of 1944/45;" a singer who was still popular until very recently has a go on the camp stage at Schubert's *Winterreise*; a professor of medicine explains "skin diseases;" a licensed engineer, "industrial effluent." There are arts and crafts afternoons for making things, sports festivals, *under the patronage of women and with coyotes keeping guard,* social evenings, and time and time again a dance.

In this ambiance, those who are demoralized at first gradually regain their old self-confidence. On the sixty-fourth weekend of his internment one of them makes the hopeful entry in his later-to-be-published diary: *Really hard work may be the game, but we still stay just the same!* After all, didn't they perform any number of heroic deeds in the field and on the Home Front? It's high time to follow that up and not sit around any longer doing nothing. On March 19, 1947, there is finally an insurrection. The inmates remove the barbed-wire barriers between the individual compounds and saw off the posts. Within minutes a veritable mass demonstration forms. *Then everyone screams "starving," as if by command, everyone, even Sepp Mayer, although he weighs over two hundred pounds and lugs along whole rolls of fat on the back of his neck. But in moments like this, he joins in the roaring like a rutting stag and bawls in solidarity, "starving."*

Most of all the inveterate National Socialists despise their political opponents and their Jewish fellow citizens who once barely managed to flee abroad in time and now dare to join forces with the odious enemy. This antipathy is, of course, mutual. Emigrants who have returned are also engaged in Glasenbach in the service of the Counter Intelligence Corps in investigating putative war criminals. The US Colonel-in-command (unarmed and alone he surrenders to the mutiny) quickly ends up in severe difficulties because of the surprising momentum of the prisoners' revolt. Guards appear, and now twelve of the CIC colleagues of Austrian origin step in to protect them, which is the height of provocation for the Nazis. *Down with the professional haters!* is one irate chant; *Gas chamber deserters!* is another.

These are verbatim quotations from the memories of one Glasenbach man, recorded on paper in 1956 without any trace of shame or even regret. The untroubled autobiographer, himself a participant in the turbulent events of March 1947, dedicates his book, by the way, to all those *who were locked up behind bars because they loved their nation and homeland more than themselves.* At any rate, the nationalist wrath has an impact. That's just what they're like, these Americans, we're derisively informed: these cowards back down if you get tough with them. The prison conditions are in fact substantially improved on the spot, the food rations are increased, and in the coming weeks many people are released to go home.

While the revolt is in full swing in Salzburg-Glasenbach,

law and justice reign supreme in St. Pantaleon. Children, for example, are strictly banned from attending the folk play rehearsed this year by the active local theater company. *The Herdswoman from the Gindl Mountain Pasture* can surely disturb the moral balance of young people. Adults, on the other hand, may make themselves comfortable for two shillings, fifty on the expensive seats in the front rows and experience up close the salacious goings on before the painted backdrop of mountains.

Not far away in Weyer, the Geratsdorfer family has in the meantime gotten back its estate. The young Maximilian, who in 1942 the Agricultural Court clearly thought too childish to be allowed to take over the paternal farm, died in battle in May of 1944. A shot through the head and chest near Sosnow cost him his life in the battle for the freedom of Greater Germany. Lieutenant Pötzlberger, the company leader, emphasizes particularly the constantly alert disposition of the dead comrade in his condolence letter to his father. Thus, his formerly disparaged character trait ensures that young Geratsdorfer still gets a funeral eulogy after all. It will, admittedly, not make any difference to him. His sister Franziska, who with her urbane manners and delicate hands also fell at that time (even if only out of official favor) will, in defiance of the existing National Socialist view of human nature, remain faithful to the farm into the next millennium.

Item four of today's session of the District Parliament in St. Pantaleon, which after the war is provisionally called the District Committee, runs as follows: *Response of the district to Kaltenberger's provisional release until the court hearing.* Such expert knowledge, requested by the wife of the interned ex-mayor, is categorically refused. But Mrs. Kaltenberger does not admit defeat so quickly. Just six weeks later the local politicians must deal anew with the vexing affair. Mayor Anton Veichtlbauer takes another vote and *the secret vote resulted in a unanimous No.* Nevertheless, it won't take long until the former head of the Women's League will have her Micky back again.

Admittedly, the district refuses categorically to give him the clean bill of health he desires, but the upstanding fellow citizen Kaltenberger, who was interned by the victors' judiciary, is so swamped by individual parties with evidence of their genuine affection that we're close to taking everything back that we were forced to declare about him up until now. At any rate, for reasons of objectivity, we have to render in the original tone what, for example, an ÖVP [Austrian People's Party] Member of the Provincial Parliament from St. Pantaleon is able to report: *I confirm that during his period of office the former District Party Group Leader and Mayor of St. Pantaleon, Michael Kaltenberger, always attended to the well-being of his district residents. My position was well known to him, and we also often talked about this. Nevertheless, I never noticed the slightest discrimination and could count on his support at all times.*

The SPÖ [Austrian Socialist Party] takes a similar view, only their local boss selects decidedly more elegiac words for the eulogy: *The undersigned confirms that Michael Kaltenberger, the then Mayor and District Party Group Leader of St. Pantaleon, has led St. Pantaleon district in an exemplary and selfless way and placed particular emphasis on clarity in his administration. His objectivity toward everyone, be they Party Comrade or non-Party member is particularly noteworthy. Although he was aware of my position as member of the SPÖ, he secured financial support for me from the Reich Agricultural Organization on the occasion of an accident in the stables.*

Of the three officially permitted parties, only the Communists are still missing. But not for long. We read, are amazed, and are silent because it takes our breath away when we discover to which of the accused's countless functions the KPÖ [Communist Party of Austria] expressly refers: *I confirm that Michael Kaltenberger always stood up for the workers. He was the Chairman of the Ibm-Waidmoos Water Cooperative and was aware of the political allegiance of many of my comrades. Despite this awareness, Kaltenberger was obliging to them in every respect, and I can only give him a positive reference.*

In the summer of 1947, Gottfried Haimbuchner, August Staudinger, and Josef Wieger are transferred from Salzburg-Glasenbach internment camp, via the camp in Pupping, to await trial in Linz. Haimbuchner, the least incriminated, finds himself released just a few weeks later, awaiting the hearing in the People's Court. Staudinger, who still has no idea why he of all people is suspected of any crimes, immediately submits a written application for release. He had to spend eight months of his custody in Glasenbach under hospital treatment; he was clearly unfit for incarceration because of his injuries. Above all, he was suffering from lapses of memory and constant headaches. A week later, August Staudinger is provisionally a free man. At the end of October, however, the court considers him for the time being sufficiently restored to be able to cope with a further period of incarceration.

His wife sees this quite differently. It's understandable that Christl Staudinger is desperate to have her husband back again immediately. First, she'd otherwise have to move out of the company's flat, she says; second, he's innocent; third, he was never in the Nazi Party; fourth, he came back home with very severe war injuries; and fifth, she's appending a number of things to her letter, such as explanations given under oath by supportive war comrades: *At the front Staudinger was always a true Austrian, and argued his point of view in the outside world by explaining his opinion regarding the Prussians. There were once even minor riots within the company because Staudinger as an Austrian railed against the fascist Hitler regime and the terrorist brown gangs and the SS. His defeatist phrases would have been sufficient then to bring him before a military court.* We can no longer inform the farm laborer Sebastian Riess, whose casual comment in 1940 about how he was in Austria and not the Third Reich resulted in serious maltreatment by August Staudinger and his immediate admission to the camp, about this admirable early change of mind because after the war the witness cannot be found.

But Christl Staudinger brings in yet bigger guns. At the end of the war in 1945, she had withdrawn with her husband to a small village at the other end of Upper Austria, where he was finally spotted by the Allies and arrested. Although August had not even lived there for a year, and nobody really knew enough about his life up to that point, anyone and everyone who had a position and a name in Laussa was of course quite willing to demand his immediate release. The priest makes a bold start with the statement: *The undersigned endorses the application wholeheartedly.* On December 7, 1947, Mrs. Staudinger then appeals to the two major parties, which state harmoniously on the same sheet of paper, complete with stamp and chairman's signature: *There is no objection from the SPÖ to the release of August Staudinger, and the application on the reverse of the page is endorsed.* The ÖVP sounds considerably more determined: *the release of August Staudinger is most urgently endorsed,* it says, even if Chairman Ferdinand Baumgartner at first mistakenly urges that a certain Friedrich Staudinger be a free man again. But wife Christl manages to spot the error in time, and the name Friedrich is deleted.

In the new year, a completely new era begins in St. Pantaleon. Henceforth, the citizens largely steer clear of the moorland; there now seems to be more than enough *Lebensraum* anyway. Instead, lignite is now being mined on a grand scale in the suburb of Trimmelkam; hundreds of industrial workers and laborers move in from all over.

Miners' colonies spring up; the unique double-shaft site quickly becomes the symbol of the region, visible far and wide. From Bürmoos a branch line eats its way through the forest and soon links both the mine and the people to the Greater Salzburg area. In one fell swoop, coal extraction and railway tracks put an end to the isolation of an area that for centuries lay in a remote border zone.

Within just a few years, the population triples and the old established rural population quickly becomes the minority; affiliations are reconfigured, and the district is forever split in two. Whereas the Socialists could be pleased up until now about having at best a single seat in the District Council in the middle of all the Conservatives, they'll soon be able to rely on a comfortable clear majority. That does not, however, have any implications for dealing with the most recent past, quite the contrary. The new rulers in the district have either recently settled here and have no feelings about the region's past, or they're long established but bear no grudges, as the phenomenal comeback of Karl Hiebler as front man for the Socialist Party will soon show. In Austria, the great public reconciliation process has long since got under way; people are only looking forward, want to create prosperity, and at all costs fill in trenches. Everything would go even faster if the Allies were not still occupying the country.

In the district offices of St. Pantaleon, a large parcel has arrived. It contains copies of the commemorative book *Never Forget!* which now already seems somewhat anachronistic. Nevertheless, it's being debated in the district committee. It is admittedly not its content that propels it up to item four of this session's agenda but solely its distribution. They agree unanimously and swiftly on a gentleman who's to sort out this tiresome business.

Six years ago, Josef, Gottfried, and August, after initially lying, finally admitted to almost everything that the

Public Prosecutor accused them of. We are going to disregard for the moment the fact that, while the deployment of rubber cudgels and Alsatian wolf-dog bites, use of pistols, and torture specialities was seemingly due to an inescapable command from above, in most cases the blame was laid on the other members of the squad. But these old files from the inquiry are not accessible at the moment – of course, the search for them is only really halfhearted, and they don't emerge again until the last guard to be convicted has long since left prison.

So the course is clear: admit only to a bare minimum. In the autumn of 1947, Josef Wieger is the first to have an opportunity to play dumb when he's questioned before the People's Court. Unfortunately, he can't recall his membership in the Nazi Party and SA that stretches back to the twenties. Yes, he was a guard in the Weyer camp, but he never maltreated anyone at all. *On the contrary, I was very popular with the inmates of the camp.* All allegations are clearly invented, wicked calumnies, he testifies, and the other SA men were also always friendly and nice. Some of the names of those who died in the camp are completely unknown to Mr. Wieger. It's a great mystery to him that the witnesses can lie so. Only right at the end of the several hours of interrogation does the adamant defendant lose his concentration. The fact that he still describes the former prisoners, apart from three members of the Hitler Youth, as dissolute and depraved characters, dulls his halo a bit.

On April 12, 1948, the late train from Germany arrives shortly after eleven in Salzburg's main station. Travelers climb wearily out of the dark green coaches, pass the customs building, and trail off into the night. One passenger would like to follow them, but he has every reason to avoid the strict border controls because he's long since been on the State Police list of people wanted for arrest. So he resolves not to leave the middle platform by the only legal exit but to disappear diagonally across the tracks.

The officials, who've initially arrested Alois Rosenbichler because he crossed the border illegally, soon know who they're dealing with. The People's Court in Linz has, after all, managed to find its main guilty party in the Weyer camp affair. The prisoners being questioned, August Staudinger and Josef Wieger, may or may not be pleased about this in their cells. A further trial is being prepared, which is expected to be the last in this matter and at the same time also the most important. We undertake to accompany Alois Rosenbichler at every turn for the next seven years. Not that we personally resent his wanting to save his own skin through all possible and impossible tricks and not that it would surprise us that his insights into his own guilt, like those of the others, will be extremely limited. To tell the truth, we won't be any more interested in Alois the individual than we have been until now.

We have neither elaborately reconstructed his childhood nor described his facial features nor crept after him into strange beds. He will himself, admittedly, soon invite us to do so; we don't know whether it's at the recommendation of the defense counsel or of his own volition. Of course, it's tempting, but we'll be brave and resist. Only where the gap between what happened and what the imaginative Alois puts on record gets too wide do we allow ourselves to raise objections. Sometimes the court will subscribe to our view.

No, the effort of tracing seven years of the Second Austrian Republic's dealings with Mr. Alois Rosenbichler is not something we're taking on because of Rosenbichler but because of the Republic. It's where we're living, and we're still moving along the course set for us earlier, wherever it may take us. As early as May 22, the very first written statement of the new prisoner awaiting trial stresses (in line with the new state's own image of itself) his role as victim: *I was admitted to the People's Court in Linz and do not know why. I do not admit at all to being guilty of an indictable offense.*

But there must, after all, have been perpetrators somewhere or other. Apparently, we weren't paying enough attention because the District Committee in St. Pantaleon had already given an impressive answer to this question some time ago. In one single sentence, meant on the surface to portray the political past of the estate manager Hans Mells as harmless, two further messages were in fact elegantly packaged: first, there's nothing particularly remarkable about a *Reichsdeutscher* having been a committed Nazi in the Third Reich, and this fact may even exonerate certain individuals, especially if they're needed in Austria and are soon naturalized. But secondly, there's a subliminal message that the Old Reich consisted almost entirely of National Socialists; that's therefore where the evil people came from, if that's how you want to see it, who drove us good people or, at worst, innocently trusting, seducible people, into disaster. Yes, that's how it must have been.

And what does the judiciary think? First of all, once the preliminary inquiries are concluded, a charge is brought against the trained bricklayer Gottfried Haimbuchner. A People's Court consists of two professional judges and three jurymen. The customary criminal proceedings system is suspended in part in Special Court proceedings. The most important feature is that there are no rights of appeal of the first court verdict. Only the Supreme Legal Court can reverse a People's Court adjudication. Up until 1955, there will be just under twenty-four thousand verdicts; fifty-eight percent read "guilty." For the guards in Weyer camp, this fraction is probably the full one hundred percent.

The proceedings against Haimbuchner ought to be particularly exciting for us; he is, after all, the only accused who was active in both camps. And furthermore, he acted as deputy to each of the bosses. We naturally know that in this courtroom it's not the Roma and Sinti that are at issue; the Republic of Austria limits itself, for whatever reasons, just like the Nazi state before it, exclusively to the events in the camp for so-called asocials. But Gottfried Haimbuchner will have to give detailed accounts of his own biography, and then somebody will probably in fact interrupt, ask questions, break the general silence.

Haimbuchner knows that only too well, and thus he callously maintains that, immediately after the closing of the Labor Education Camp, he arranged a prolonged holiday. In February 1942, he was then sent to Waldegg to work in a Gypsy Detention Camp as financial manager. Anyhow, the key word has come up. We observe with satisfaction that the Public Prosecutor insists on being allowed to speak. Now he will say right away: My dear Mr. Haimbuchner, so you went on holiday for thirteen months, right in the middle of the war? Is your memory not playing a trick on you there?

Far off the mark – Dr. Hauser is much more interested in the accused's illegal membership in the NSDAP during the Austrian *Ständestaat*. We, on the other hand, would like to ask: Does the name Rudolf Haas still mean anything to you? He was a really small, completely dead Gypsy; he'd be only seven years old now. Does the strange cause of death "too weak to live" mean anything to you, a diagnosis confirmed by a certain Gottfried Haimbuchner, Weyer Deputy Camp Director, right in the middle of the well-earned, long-term holiday? Speak up, man!

Instead, the accused admits that he had been registered in the SA and Nazi Party as early as 1933. Nor does he deny that on the day of the *Anschluss*, together with his men at home in Pischelsdorf, he occupied the district offices and police station, demanded the key to the cash box, and uttered threats. Apart from that, however, he does not plead guilty. Admittedly, he joined in the Christmas beating; that much is true, but in an understandable state of agitation about the victim.

It was like this, Your Honor, is how Haimbuchner defends himself: the prisoner, Edmund Haller, received a summons in the camp to appear at the Wildshut District Court. It was, I believe, a matter of alimony. Camp Commandant Staudinger did not want to let him leave the camp, but when the boss was away, I, being a good chap, let Haller go on his solemn promise to return. Then August Staudinger returned unexpectedly, and I got into trouble over this. He then had Haller brought back immediately by the police.

The Christmas gift-giving didn't take place till weeks later, but Gottfried was still understandably excited. Indeed, as far as he could remember, it was Alois Rosenbichler and Josef Mayrlehner, in other words two low-ranking subordinates, who ordered him, poor Gottfried, to join in the beating, which he at first obstinately resisted, but to no avail. But then Haller of all people joined him, and on account of the excitement, oh well. Yet afterwards Haimbuchner immediately inquired whether it had in fact hurt, and Edmund Haller said no. A few weeks before the start of the trial, the witness unfortunately passed away.

Far away from home, Gottfried Haimbuchner wants to begin a new life after the war. With a wife and two small children, the now forty-nine year old is living contentedly as a hard-working and honest laborer, except for a break of one year in Glasenbach internment camp and a few weeks of detention awaiting trial in Linz. These periods are also counted towards his sentence of fifteen months, because the former SA Storm Trooper is guilty, in the court's earnest belief, but the proceedings against the main perpetrators are still to come. Gottfried Haimbuchner may go. Nobody will ever question him about the fate of the Romanies.

In June 1948, August Staudinger begins to find detention awaiting trial boring. Despite all the endeavors of his spouse, the judiciary simply doesn't want to let the former Weyer camp commandant go, as his war comrades, his priest, and the major parties all expect. Quite the contrary, the trial will actually take place this year; that's anticipated. August senses that nothing good will come of it. So one day he quietly and secretly takes leave of his poorly guarded place of work and moves abroad. He means to spend the winter there until the rest of Austria also comes round to his rock-solid conviction that he had been, at the most, somewhat too zealous in a few details.

Now it's Josef Wieger's turn. In his trial, a large number of former witnesses are called to testify for the first time. But in the meantime, their ranks have dwindled considerably. We don't want to imagine for ourselves how many people's frank words in front of the Nazi interrogation authorities were their undoing after the Führer called off the proceedings in 1942. Preferential deployment to the front, concentration camps, harassment of all types are conceivable. Dozens of summons delivered as registered letters come back with the note "deceased" or "unknown" to the disappointed sender, the People's Court. Admittedly, some copies of witness statements from 1941 have, as we have learned in the meantime, been preserved in police stations; it will be possible to fall back on them if required. In contrast, the inquiry files of the Public Prosecutor's Office are still missing.

Kirchschlag is a common place name in this country;

in Upper Austria, there is one just beyond Linz. Kirchschlag is where the farmer Ludwig Steffel is supposed to have come from, the man who experienced a lot in the camp, not least the ominous Christmas punishment, strapped down naked on a bench. The Public Prosecutor would have liked to have had a chat with him. In Kirchschlag, they don't know of anyone called Steffel; in fact, there's never been one there. If the box files from 1941 were available, it would be easy to establish that the farmer Steffel's Kirchschlag was in Oberdonau all right but not in Upper Austria. It's now called Svetlik in South Bohemia, beautifully situated high above a bend in the Moldava river, and if he's survived the Third Reich and the dispossession, other worries will probably be plaguing Mr. Steffel at present. In the end, the Czechs, understandably but nevertheless unfairly, don't want to have anything at all to do with the Sudeten Germans anymore and don't care much whether the people in question were Nazi victims themselves or not. We can confidently assume that farmer Steffel has lost his farm in the meantime, and if nothing worse has happened, has found a temporary refuge somewhere in Germany or Austria.

The authorities also summon a certain Ludwig Kriechbauer; the man is also said to have been severely maltreated in the Weyer Labor Education Camp. In Steyr they pull out all the stops but have to report that despite an intensive search they've not managed to turn up anyone of that name. They're at a loss as to what's happened to him. Ludwig Kriechbauer is one of those who died in the camp and is said to have been lying since 1940 in an unmarked grave in the Bavarian cemetery at Laufen on the Salzach. Of course, all of that had been ascertained long ago, but the People's Court proceedings will, under the circumstances, have to start turning up the evidence again because of the serious gaps in the files. Speaking of starting again, no earthly court will be able to bring suit against the *spiritus rector* behind the whole affair, NS multi-functionary Franz Kubinger; he too is no longer in the land of the living.

On July 2, 1948, the chief accused, Alois Rosenbichler, is interrogated at length. The former SA Senior Staff Sergeant declares, as expected, that he has at no time been a member of a NS organization. He could swear on oath that he never made an application to join the SA. Of course, as one of the guards and instructors in the camp, he did wear the appropriate brown uniform for a few days, but he definitely was not part of the Nazi apparatus, that's for sure.

To be precise, during that time, in fact for only a total of three weeks, he hardly belonged to the SA Guard Team in Weyer at all. As far as the accusations are concerned, he either had absolutely nothing whatsoever to do with their actions or acted under extreme duress. Of course, Alois focuses on his superiors, the elusive August Staudinger and especially the dead comrade Josef Mayrlehner. The few instances of maltreatment which Rosenbichler, when pressed, does in the end acknowledge, were, he says, only committed because the Camp Commandant himself threatened him so strongly. Also, it was only a question of a few boxed ears at most. Rubber cudgels, service pistols, hobnailed hiking boots? Never heard about that.

Then Dr. Hofer, who's leading the questioning, would actually like things a bit more precise. Let's talk about the Christmas distribution of gifts. *In his capacity as my superior, Staudinger gave me the task, with the comment that I was the youngest, of issuing 25 blows to the backside with the rubber cudgel to about 5 or 6 prisoners in the presence of inmates in the camp canteen, after presents had been given to the other prisoners. After my initial reluctance, Staudinger and Wieger gave me the official command that I had to carry out this chastisement. Staudinger now had the prisoners selected for beating stretched out individually over a bench, and I had* to inflict in each case either 5, 10, 15, or 25 blows with the rubber cudgel to the buttocks of the person in question. Staudinger supervised the whole event. Too bad for poor Alois that August Staudinger and Josef Wieger had, as the record showed, taken Christmas leave on that day.

And the business with Josef Mayer? Do you still remember? He suddenly remembers. Alois Rosenbichler knows intimately how he was called to the room by a worried prisoner because Mayer was fighting with some others. *I made my way to this room and wanted to challenge Maier about his behavior. Maier was a tall, strong man, about 45 years old. But instead of giving any answer, Maier attacked me straight away; he grabbed me by the neck and spat in my face. Of course, I wasn't putting up with that and knocked him down. In doing so, I made use of my rubber cudgel, dealing him about 3 - 4 blows to the buttocks. After I had wrestled Maier down, I pulled him by the shoulders from the room into the porch. There I didn't hit him any more, but just told him he should be sensible and not get into scuffles in the room and should refrain from spitting in my face again; he would always draw the shorter straw if he did. That was the extent of my involvement with Maier. What the prisoners then did with Maier I never knew.*

Let's drop by now for a few minutes at the trial of Josef Wieger, which is taking place just a week later. Whether he's guilty or not is something he doesn't know. This is Josef's initial sheepish opinion. His bold statements made during the questioning a few months previously could in fact in the meantime almost all be refuted. That hurts. Now only the compassion trick can help: *I do not remember ever having stated anything like that. I received a head wound in the First World War and often forget everything.* On being questioned he said: *Nobody was beaten; at most I gave someone a shove.* After an exhaustive account of events, he stated: *Now and again I clouted a prisoner with my hand.* On being pressed to go into detail: *Nobody was beaten till they bled and very definitely not by me. I also admit that we as guards had rubber tubing, but I only hit people with it on the back or the buttocks.*

Bit by bit, Josef Wieger grudgingly acknowledges with no trace of regret what the many witnesses unanimously declare. That lands him in jail for two and a quarter years. The accused, like Gottfried Haimbuchner, has to live in the future with the fact of having been legally convicted of war crimes. Admittedly, the low level of intelligence of the accused was seen as an extenuating circumstance in determining the punishment. That is surprising; Mr. Wieger is after all a qualified master cobbler, was for a time a civilian workshop manager in the army, and after his activities as an educator in Weyer he was Camp Director in the weekday camp of the Linz shipyard, an altogether respectable career for someone bordering on the moronic. Further mitigating circumstances to be considered, in addition to his inferior rank, were the fact that other guard personnel were even worse, and that in individual cases Wieger helped relatives of camp inmates.

At the end of September, a notification arrives at the Linz Federal Police Headquarters from the Federal Ministry of the Interior, which at the same time is passed on to all Security authorities in Austria for their careful attention: *84.426 – 4/48. Ref: Gypsy plague.* The Director General for Public Security wishes to announce: *It has come to the notice of the head office that the Gypsy plague is once again threatening in some areas of the federal territory and is already attracting attention. In order to make an impression on the Austrians, the Gypsies are said to be passing themselves off as concentration camp prisoners and victims.*

Because the requirements of police regulations concerning foreigners appear to be met, and the possibility of getting them out of the country *exists, a residence ban should be issued against troublesome Gypsies and their removal effected.* If that can't be done because these people have Austrian papers, then at least their travel movements should be watched closely. The departure of individuals or the movement of groups from one area to another is to be watched and the authorities notified.

We are downright grateful to the Honorable Director General for the refreshingly open use of a word, which, though it seems fuzzy, and therefore in fact unusable in the new Austrian state, has stood the test of time in the Austrian new constitution as hardly any other has: *troublesome.* People can be anything they like, just not troublesome. Is there anything possibly worse than troublesome children or critics? What could pose a more lasting threat to public safety than troublesome individuals of whatever sort? It's just troublesome that tried and tested means of preventing this, which until very recently could be applied without any qualms, are at the moment only possible within a certain framework: removal from the country. That's right, but just not to Lodz; tight supervision, yes, but just not behind walls and barbed wire.

Karl Gumpelmaier, who eight years ago, as we recall, did not want to purchase a German Labor Front flag for his firm, survived the Labor Education Camp severely scarred. So he is also supposed to make a statement as a witness at the imminent trial of Alois Rosenbichler. The People's Court, however, receives a letter in response to the summons sent out within the correct period of time, in which Karl Gumpelmaier, Junior, lets us know the following: *My father died in February 1947 of a heart complaint that he developed in the winter of 1940/41 in the St. Pantaleon camp. My father's testimony, which he gave in April 1941 at the police station in Mauthausen, ought to still be there. My mother still possesses a copy of this statement, but we do not want to let that out of our hands since we are seeking support for my mother through*

Victim Relief and need supporting documents for this.

Are we getting bogged down in details, in which, as they say, the devil dwells? May we give in to the temptation to quote whole pages verbatim when we have in fact undertaken to recount things simply and as concisely as possible, as it was, as it is? So let's be strict with ourselves; let's content ourselves from now on with the knowledge that we could if we wanted.

Alois Rosenbichler's lawyer sensitively guides the hand of his client when the latter submits an application for release on October 13, 1948. What has he to propose in support of his case? Oh yes, the compulsion to obey orders, the short period spent working in the camp, only three weeks instead of the ten that all the others remember. And above all: *During the period I served there, I never maltreated anyone or offended their human dignity.* In this respect, he once was more open, was good old Alois.

It will soon be seven years or, as the case may be, three months, since the respective interrogations, and things are so quickly forgotten in these confused times, even if there isn't a bullet wound to the head to be invoked, as in the case of many of the old comrades. Besides, Alois Rosenbichler has been infamous since time immemorial for the fact that none of his statements are valid beyond the day in question. As early as 1941, the irritated Public Prosecutor notes in the minutes that Rosenbichler's account was a very changeable one. At one point, he would, for example, admit that he used rubber cudgels, then he would roundly deny charges to that effect.

But further on in the text of the application for release: there was no danger he would try to flee, since it could not be assumed that he would want to avoid responsibility by fleeing. Aha. But that's by no means the end of it. Then there's the chronic stomach complaint, enhanced by what was then diagnosed as an acute stomach ulcer, which was why he was dismissed from the army in 1940, and consequently his reliance on special diet foods which the prison unfortunately does not provide. After all, as an innocent prisoner under investigation, he cannot hold down a job and is therefore suffering a great financial loss as a result. That in turn exposes his decrepit seventy-two-year-old father to extreme distress because he, Alois, has to look after him. Apparently, and this is really how we must interpret the concerns of a grateful son, the aged man had nobody else left who could make the difficult twilight years of his life tolerable. The court declines to release him and two weeks later sends the lawyer the indictment.

We'd already reached this point once before. Only now there's no longer an Adolf Hitler to dismiss such proceedings, no August Eigruber as Gauleiter moving heaven and earth so that the Führer turns his attention to the matter, no Stefan Schachermayr as Regional Inspector who threatens the Public Prosecutor and makes documents vanish, but only one Stefan Schachermayr, a salesman from Wels, released recently after three years in prison, who is a witness in the case against Alois Rosenbichler.

We move inconspicuously into the courtroom now, where the main hearing is set for the seventeenth of January, 1949. The accused, Alois Rosenbichler, is charged with leaving countless inmates of the Weyer Education Camp in an excruciating state and having maltreated them, actions which resulted in grave violations of the dignity of man and the laws of humanity, and which furthermore led to the death of at least two victims. In short, he committed the crime of torture and maltreatment as defined in the pertinent law code.

The accused explains that he was not guilty, and right at the start, he dumbfounds those present with the assertion that not only did he not maltreat anyone, but he himself often joined in the work so that the quotas could be met. He was actually, this is what he seems to want to tell us, he was himself indeed, what's the right word? A victim, yes, a victim. The defense counsel uses this favorable opportunity to divert the attention of the room to the impoverished childhood of his client, who now for the first time recites the well-rehearsed legend of his family of eighteen. From now on, we will be hearing this repeatedly, until December 4, 1954, when the Ostermiething police station informs the District Authority in Braunau, regarding the question of whether Alois Rosenbichler should be shown mercy, that the latter has seven brothers and sisters of whom five are still alive.

But it is not only with eighteen family members that the accused attempts to impress the authorities but also with the fact that he was banished from home by his brutal father at the tender age of twelve years and in his youth received more blows than meals. Three months ago, the same Mr. Rosenbichler wanted to be released immediately, on the grounds that it was absolutely essential that he, the exemplary and apparently only son, had to care for his old, fragile father. But meanwhile his reputation as a loving child has become legally worthless. His lawyer is definitely of the opinion that a lost youth under a brute of a father is unambiguously the better mitigating circumstance.

Even the chronic stomachache played its role. No more talk about inadequate food supplies in the prison. No, he had had to resign his post at that time and suffer in the camp as a guard because of a war injury that became more severe in the coming years with each request for mercy. He never touched the internees, not even Mayer. As for the statements made during interrogation, he retracts them. *It is not quite clear to me why the prisoners so maltreated Mayer.*

In the next day and a half, twenty-eight people in total enter the witness box, former guards, former camp prisoners, and civilian workers for the Water Authority, ex-NS-functionaries, doctors, lawyers. The accused hopes in vain for a single defense witness. Even the old insider networks have become shredded. Alois Rosenbichler must actually be pleased if those people who previously called the shots say nothing.

The former Regional Inspector Stefan Schachermayr, for example, who was instrumental in the selection of a candidate list in the VdU [League of Independents] election campaign for the parliamentary elections did not at that time, in 1940-41, apparently know at all what was actually going on. He only went to the camp in order to be able at least to give the Gauleiter an authentic report. The latter wanted to avoid legal proceedings whatever happened, because Himmler had already been opposed to the camp in any case. And furthermore, for Eigruber's taste, the Public Prosecutor questioned far too many people from the area round the camp who were opposed to National Socialism. Ultimately, the Gauleiter merely wanted to prevent the bad conditions in this camp from being exaggerated. This is actually what Schachermayr says in the end. Whether Kubinger ordered the maltreatment is likewise not known to the witness, but he is obliged to say that he would not have put that past him. He himself, as mentioned, knew nothing at all or at best somehow indirectly. We're also writing this down word for word, because it's just too good.

The accused feels he is caught up in an evil plot. The statements of one witness are, in his eyes, a complete pack of lies; the assertion of another is simply false. The statements of a third witness are not in accordance with the facts; *I did not have a blackjack in my possession and only needed such a weapon once.* The fourth witness's assertion is a pack of lies; what the fifth witness says is not in accordance with the truth. The sixth witness *bears hatred towards me because of a relationship between his daughter and me. Witness: I never bore hatred towards the accused. Accused: But he did towards my grandfather.* A seventh witness recalls: *The accused once said, If only the time would finally come when you could be shot. Accused: I never said that.*

Josef Wieger has already served his sentence because his imprisonment and detention awaiting trial were counted in full. He says that he warned Alois repeatedly about his brutality although he in his own proceedings six months previously emphatically denied ever having seen any acts of violence committed by his colleagues. Instead, the present accused denies just as adamantly ever having been given a warning by Josef. Gottfried Haimbuchner has likewise been summoned as a witness and admits that the guards were equipped with rubber cudgels and also frequently used them. In contrast to him, Alois really looked forward for days to the Christmas gift-giving. The latter fundamentally denies the pleasure and, with only one exception, resolutely denies the use of rubber cudgels. But for the first time, he dimly recalls that they had all occasionally used garden hoses for the same purposes.

The big exception is the Christmas chastisement. Alois unreservedly admits to it; he did beat people until he himself was quite exhausted. But just note, your honor: Camp Commander Staudinger stood alongside; you understand, it was a clear case of forcing us to obey orders. The court has heard enough and withdraws for consultations.

In the name of the Republic, the accused is guilty. He has to listen to quite a number of grounds for the verdict: in view of the autopsy records, his statement that he only gave Anton Atzelsberger a few light blows round the ear was ludicrous. It was almost certain that he was also responsible for other deaths, but it should be acknowledged that the relevant causal connections cannot be deemed proven beyond a doubt. Many files had unfortunately disappeared, including an early confession by the accused in the Josef Mayer case. The fact that he frankly acknowledged the actions on the occasion of the Christmas chastisement with which he was charged, because he thought that Staudinger's command exonerated him, shows just how little faith can be put in the rest of his denials. It had been proven only that Camp Director Staudinger was on holiday, but even if he had ordered the mistreatment, it would have been an easy matter for the accused to soften the punishment. For *it must be said in this regard that orders can be carried out in a variety of ways, even if they cannot be circumvented. What the accused did in this case has, however, to be seen as a crime in the sense of §3 of the War Crimes Law.*

We can breathe again. The People's Court confirms to us in 51 detailed pages that everything happened just as we have described. Cold-bloodedly, sadistically, and brutally was how Alois Rosenbichler proceeded, but the death penalty would not be imposed due to mitigating circumstances. At this point, there follow the eighteen-member family of his childhood, the brutal father, a certain pressure from above, and once again the low level of intelligence of the accused. He's sentenced to fifteen years in prison, with the extra penalty of solitary confinement without food or water every twenty-fourth of December.

The conclusion for the time being of proceedings in the Weyer matter – there's still a warrant out for the arrest of Camp Boss August Staudinger – prompts us to make observations about what was actually at stake in the trials against the dreadful team of educators. In contrast to their colleagues in the Third Reich, the Austrian public prosecutors are exclusively interested in actual acts of violence.

The People's Court rules on war crimes; no light is thrown on the structures of Nazi governance, as in the instance of the Labor Education Camp. Those who are prosecuted, if any, are individual perpetrators, who as a rule have no regrets and regard themselves as political prisoners. The People's Court trials are not linked to a social mandate.

Therefore, what they fail to mention are reviews of crucial matters like the reasons and circumstances for admission to the camp; completely omitted are the many cunning, desk-bound National Socialists at middle-level and below, who outlawed harmless contemporaries and unscrupulously profited by the suffering of others, who ensured that incriminating documents disappeared in time, and who tell whopping lies whenever they open their mouths.

Naturally, we have also, for example, heard Michael Kaltenberger today in the witness box, the landlord who was dismissed even before Christmas 1947. He explained verbatim that mayors like himself hadn't had anything to do with admissions to the camp; that had been the responsibility of the employment offices. That's not true, as we know. But nobody says it to his face or says it to the many people across the whole country who in 1949 still think, or once again think, that Hitler himself did not know anything about the concentration camps. In the end, such people believe that the highways ought to be on the credit side of the ledger as well as the disempowerment of Jewish capitalists.

That's how it comes about that, years after the end of the war, camp victims, their children, and their widows – like, for example, the wife of one Karl Gumpelmaier – still have to try under extremely difficult circumstances to scratch together the necessary documentation that would justify awards from the Victim Relief Fund. It probably wasn't as bad as all that is what people will all too often say to them, or it probably was not completely without reason that they locked you or your husband up. Certainly, it's also only carelessness on the part of the reporter for the *Upper Austrian News* when he writes about the ninety-minute proceedings in which Alois Rosenbichler had to account for himself, instead of a one-and-a-half-day trial lasting a good eleven hours. But it is nevertheless symptomatic: the fact that there was probably not much to dispute in these meager ninety minutes confirms many a reader's verdict on the victors' justice, and after that the poor guy gets a sentence of fifteen years imposed on him.

At the end of the 1940s, the hundred and fifty kilometers to Linz are still an onerous journey. Countless witnesses in the proceedings against Alois Rosenbichler give the hamlets of Loidersdorf, Laubenbach, or Wildshut, or the largest village in the district, St. Pantaleon itself, as their place of residence. Time and time again in past years, they have been summoned to the capital and reported truthfully in one of the People's Courts what happened on the site of Nazi terror at the outermost edge of the Austrian state.

This time the front page of the *New Watch on the Inn* carries the headline *Aftermath of the Infamous SA Labor Camp in Weyer.* It's January 20, 1949. The detailed report of the trial culminates in two details, which for the visibly shocked journalist throw a particularly significant light on the events of that time. Thus a witness who survived both camps concluded his testimony with the incredible assertion *that it had not been as bad in Mauthausen concentration camp as in that camp in Weyer.* And: *in his concluding speech Public Prosecutor Dr. Eigenbauer pointed out that there had not yet been a trial in the People's Court where NOT ONE SINGLE EXONERATING WITNESS had testified.*

The memory of the camp must therefore still be vivid in the village, and so we then assume that the honorable group which agrees in 1949 that the sorrow over the deaths in the Second World War would go beyond the scope of the existing war memorial at least does not completely ignore those unfortunate people who fell victim to the SA's torture. Something new, large, and impressive is what's needed; after a few debates a memorial committee is formed that has the task of organizing and raising a fund. The scheme is to be financed entirely by donations, but it soon runs into problems. Everything begins to cost more than planned, and the donations are rather disappointing. So the district reluctantly accepts responsibility for the sum still outstanding, expecting that the money will surely turn up some time, somehow, from somewhere. The district doctor, Dr. Straffner, votes against this and wants people to face up to realities. He develops a straightforward four-point scheme, which is finally approved by a majority of the District Council. First: the memorial committee is disbanded. Second: the district takes over the bills and settles them immediately in order at least to save interest on the overdue penalties. Third: even the sculptor gets the last installment of his fee at once. Fourth: the treasurer of the former memorial committee has to present a report immediately.

During these years, Dr. Straffner not only proposes the most successful motions at meetings of the District Parliament but also delivers the most speeches, and is regularly kind enough to read aloud the minutes of the previous meeting. His influence in the People's Party is great; as far as the work of remembering is concerned, he is without a doubt the right man in the right place. We are already picturing his next ambitious four-point scheme, this time for the content of the memorial's design. First: a monument like that has to emphasize the victimization of those who met a violent death under Nazi rule. The great majority of the fallen and missing definitely did not see themselves as heroic figures. Second: I know best how the Weyer camp deaths came about. I can still today see before my eyes the appalling images of those who were tortured to death, and indeed not just when I'm standing once again in the witness box of the Linz People's Court. We will, I propose, have the names of these unfortunate people engraved on the monument, together with those of the fallen soldiers. Third: we former NS local politicians – and I'm probably not the only one in this room who has painful memories of that – during the Third Reich we proceeded, according to official recommendations, to assign handicapped people to institutions like Castle Hartheim, where they then became victims of a program of euthanasia. When I agreed to intern the eleven-year-old Hermann Kronberger there without delay, I did not, of course, yet know anything about these crimes. We then moved on without long discussion to the next item on the agenda: whether St. Pantaleon should join in the Ostermiething warehouse co-operative. We now know that Hermann didn't survive his imprisonment; his name is on the unbearably long list of those who died in Hartheim. It will also be on our monument. Fourth: we in St. Pantaleon, of all people involved, have particular reason to say "never, ever again." There will surely be enough room on our monument for these words.

Bravo. The applause after this impressive speech is long and loud. We imagine that right away another local politician immediately will raise his hand to speak, clear his throat and argue that it was absolutely essential that even those St. Pantaleon children who perhaps did not fall in battle six kilometers before Kiev or did not have Grave Number 168 in the heroes' cemetery one kilometer east of Piacenza, but who died in the ghetto in Litzmannstadt or were gassed in Kulmhof and were cremated anonymously, should also be mentioned by name on the monument. He had taken the trouble and already drawn their dates from the registry of births, the people's representative says proudly. Just a moment, for a start there's a certain Maria Leimberger, born on February 16, 1941, in the camp in Weyer, daughter of Mathilde Leimberger and Josef Lichtenberger, both Gypsies and camp prisoners. Then Rudolf Haas, born on April 8, 1941, in the camp in Weyer, son of Maria Haas and Josef Steiner, both Gypsies and camp prisoners; this infant actually died later in the camp, as I see here, and was buried somewhere over there in Haigermoos. Furthermore, Eduard Demestra, born on the first of September, 1941, in the camp at Weyer, son of Marie Demestra and Martin, I can't read his full name now. Anyway, the mother's a Gypsy and was interned here at this time; the father was a basket weaver of unknown address. Then we have here little Konrad Kerndlbacher, born on the seventh of September, 1941, in the camp in Weyer, son of Theresia Kerndlbacher and Hermann Kugler, both Gypsies and camp prisoners. And finally one Marie Held, born on the eighteenth of October, 1941, in the camp in Weyer, daughter of Juliana Held and Iwan Blach, both Gypsies; she was interned in Weyer, he of unknown address. What do you say to my proposal?

Nothing is what they say because of course we wait in vain for a discussion of Gypsies. Even Dr. Straffner is unfortunately not going to take any stand on these cases. So the discussion is confined exclusively to the tribute to fallen and missing soldiers, as is customary in this country. When *these heroes are immortalized in a new war memorial*, as the local chronicle proudly reports thirty years later, a life-size, naturalistic bronze figure (we've anticipated it) adorns the monument: a soldier who has just been wounded sinks to his knees and breathes the last breath of his young life. *I*

Had a Comrade is written in large Gothic script below him, and even one Josef Mayr is to be found in the chiselled list of war victims, but it's not the man of almost the same name with the pumpkin-sized testicles who lies buried a few meters away without a cross.

After a decent interval (we suspected this would happen), a good quarter of the members of the NS District Council were returned in the last election to the District Parliament. For example, Dr. Alois Straffner and Hans Mells from the Austrian People's Party are seated opposite the socialist Karl Hiebler. Even Michael Kaltenberger is back again, but only today on this fifth of April, and as a guest. At this time, he's not performing any official functions, apart, that is, from the office of Deputy Squad Leader of the Potato Beetle Tracking Service. First of all, the village landlord would like to fill people in on the status of his still-pending proceedings regarding the war criminal charge. He does indeed have very good prospects, but it would really be nice if the gentlemen from the district committee were to provide a character reference for the Public Prosecutor that corresponds to the truth, were such a reference, contrary to expectations, to be requested. *It is inconceivable to him that he could be described in the official 1947 character reference as a fanatical Nazi. Admittedly, he was a convinced National Socialist but never fanatical.* Kaltenberger's report is noted, and then it's on to the next item on the agenda, the *application to appoint a monument warden to be permanently in charge of the St. Pantaleon war memorial.*

No, we really can't go on hoping any more. Now we're fighting the Cold War, not the hot one; the ranks are closing from now on against the red peril from the east; in Austria, the major parties, as well as the newly founded Independent Alliance, in which the former Regional Inspector Stefan Schachermayr is investing all his energies, are wooing the considerable pool of voters formed by the recently denazified, former Nazi Party Comrades; even in St. Pantaleon, there are large-scale celebrations for the returning veterans, to which we would not have the slightest objection if they did not have a dubious aura. And when a new Federal President has to be elected because Karl Renner dies in office, Alois Rosenbichler (a good two years after his conviction still in the men's penitentiary in Garsten) sees that his hour has come. For the first time, we look over his shoulder as he writes and are somewhat surprised; his handwriting is anything but spiky and clumsy, as his educational background and the court's low rating of his intelligence as grounds for exoneration would suggest, but proficient, fluent, smooth, and extremely neat. Even if we suspect that the actual author of the lines to the People's Court was his lawyer, it's still striking that every sentence, every word, every comma is accurate.

Mr. Rosenbichler wants to go home; he has had enough of the monotony of the penitentiary and justifies his emotional state as follows: *1.) The Honorable Federal Minister for Justice has pointed out in a speech on the occasion of the Honorable Federal President's assumption of office that he considers the time has come to issue a pardon also to those people who at the time fell afoul of the law for political reasons and to draw a line under the political past of the individual.* Alois Rosenbichler, who claims never to have been a member of the NSDAP, the SA, or any other NS group, can thus still not come to terms with his status as a convicted violent criminal. He still sees himself as a political prisoner who is doing time simply because of an ethos which he once supported unconditionally, often admittedly affecting other people as well.

At some point in the last months, a woman from Germany, who had previously searched in vain for the man who had gone into hiding, must have got in touch with him in the penitentiary. If Alois had in fact known earlier what he now knows, he surely would indeed have played this trump card at the trial: *2.) I have an illegitimate son, Alois, born on May 1, 1940, whom I should look after, but this is impossible because of my imprisonment. Since I am very attached to the child, this is sorely troubling my conscience.* Towards the end, Alois, Sr., sprinkles in a generous pinch of contrition, when he frankly admits *that at that time, in my youthful ignorance, I went too far.*

Despite these convincing arguments, the People's Court does not want to act right away since Mr. Rosenbichler has only served a tiny fraction of his sentence. So three months later, Alois takes up his pen again and addresses the man who is his greatest hope, the new socialist Federal President Theodor Körner. *I am encouraged to do this by statements made by leading Austrian political and public figures, which recently have been appearing more and more frequently in the press, statements to the effect that a line must be drawn under the problem of Nazi and war crimes.* Alois Rosenbichler ventures his request *in view of the imminent Christmas celebration, taking into account the political stabilization.*

In the meantime, word about the advanced political stabilization has even spread as far as August Staudinger in his German exile. Around Christmas time, the ever-patriotic Austrian is evidently suffering from severe homesickness in the young Federal Republic; on January 4, 1952, the Linz People's Court receives the surprise written notification that this elusive man is henceforth inclined to return. *To this end, I submit my request for the trial to be arranged as soon as possible, namely, at a time convenient for my defense counsel, if possible on January 14, 1952.*

Before the Public Prosecutor, to whom a copy of the document is conveyed, can fully recover from his astonishment at the bold proposal of a date, he's already captivated by the considerably bolder requests to produce evidence, which are attached to this request. In them, Mr. Staudinger refers to the charge brought against him four years previously. Gaps in memory due to war injuries are out of the question; in fact, the accused recalls clearly that everything was completely different. In consultation with his lawyer, he envisages as main witnesses in his defense Messrs. Stefan Schachermayr, ex-Regional Inspector of the NSDAP; Franz Stadlbauer, ex-Regional Chairman of the German Labor Front; and the landlord and Ex-District Party Group Leader Michael Kaltenberger. And what, in his opinion, are all the many things the old comrades can swear to?

For example, first, in fact it wasn't me, poor old August, who was the Camp Director at all, *but a certain Franz Kubinger, who was an SA Mayor.* Kubinger's dead as a dodo; it can't hurt him anymore that Mr. Staudinger doesn't exactly remember the old terms for the ranks is what he wants to convey to us indirectly; anyway, he never identified with that stuff, and as a precaution the Mayor is mentioned again immediately so that it doesn't look like a typing error.

For example, second, the majority of the people admitted were criminal and asocial creatures, which is why it's understandable that one's patience might have been tested. *With absolute certainty* the good man remembers that *Rössler, Kreil, and Riess, the persons presented as harmless fathers of families and considerate husbands, are creatures with serious previous convictions.* With absolute certainty, we can, on the other hand, announce that all of these three gentlemen were single. Mr. Rössler, about whose, allegedly criminal, previous life nothing is known, died later in a concentration camp; Mr. Kreil was a harmless eighteen-year-old apprentice with no previous conviction whatsoever and is now once again a respected citizen. Mr. Riess's trail was finally lost in the Second World War, and he too was indeed questioned in detail about personal data when he gave evidence in 1941, yet was not exposed as a habitual criminal. A few months before his flight (may August Staudinger forgive us this irritating infatuation with detail), on November 14, 1947, the accused actually said verbatim, in the context of an interrogation, in response to the relevant allegations: *The witness Rössler is unknown to me. I do not know the witness Riess.* But at the time, the man was still plagued by massive memory gaps.

For example, third, many prisoners had confirmed August's irreproachable behavior, and no maltreatment at all could have taken place in Room 20 because there hadn't been twenty rooms in all for the thirty inmates. We only note in passing that the average number of prisoners was generally three times as high, but there were actually not sleeping quarters for twenty in the first camp; when he's right, he's right. On the other hand, room numbers in accommodations like hotels or educational institutions often obey their own rules: the number one, for example, usually stands for the first floor, and room thirteen can easily be followed one floor higher by room twenty.

To cut short a long list of requests to produce evidence: apart from a few harmless boxes on the ears for monstrous, highly dangerous criminals by a simple but overworked guard, there's nothing, but really nothing at all. And so, dear People's Court, we're best advised to talk about that in the courtroom as friends in, let's say, ten days, so that we can swiftly put this exasperating business behind us. Agreed?

Whether or not there's stabilization, that's an imposition, even for the most hardened judge. The requested schedule is politely dismissed; the feeling is that, apart from the witnesses proposed by Staudinger, the court also still wants to hear others; it will even take the time to interrupt the trial in March for four weeks in order to summon further people who participated in the events. August Staudinger is genuinely disappointed about such provocative demands of a judicial bureaucracy gone crazy, which obviously lacks a strong hand to regulate it. And thus during the hearing, he has to face the serious allegation from the policeman from his native Prambachkirchen that our upright Austrian patriot arrested him during the *Anschluss* on the night of the thirteenth of March, 1938, at two o'clock in the morning and locked him up in the district jail; and what's more, he was in SA uniform although Staudinger had said that he'd not in fact joined till later and had only had himself backdated illegally in order to further his career prospects. Before the invasion, he was only a member of the German Gymnastics Association. With regard to the later grounds for the verdict, we also wish to note that the Ex-Camp-Boss explains once again verbatim at the beginning of his account that he did not maltreat anybody; only *now and then, when it was necessary, did he give an insubordinate prisoner a box on the ears.*

From the perspective of the witnesses, of course, these facts sound more like this in the course of the trial: *Right away he hit me in the face twice with 5 to 6 blows, until he knocked me down. Bled from the nose and had a black eye for 14 days. He beat me so badly that I was unconscious and they carried me out. After ten minutes I came to my senses again.* The court sums up the essence of the conclusion from the evidence as follows: *Thus each newcomer was beaten right away by none other than the accused, Staudinger, in the camp office.* There follows a long list of examples: punches, kicks, beatings with the rubber cudgel. Much blood was said to have flowed and the maltreated had not been able to work for up to four days afterward. Given these unambiguous statements, the somewhat surprising conclusion *that his assaults were not particularly rough and above all in no case resulted in severe injuries for those affected* is worth its weight in gold for the accused.

Staudinger now still sees light at the end of the tunnel after all. The fact that he was, after all, the Camp Commandant in Weyer is completely irrelevant for the People's Court in 1952. The fact that there were a series of dreadfully beaten dead people in the area for which he was responsible, that he didn't draw obvious conclusions from that, didn't report a single subordinate, or at least verifiably discipline him, but, on the contrary, did all in his power to obstruct the judiciary in its enquiries, what the hell. If you were perhaps to follow the logic of the guilty verdict in the trial of Josef Wieger, whose *subordinate position held in the camp* was credited to his account in mitigation, Staudinger's position of power, proven beyond any doubt, would have to be seen as making him more responsible. But that's very wide of the mark. *According to the contention of the charge, the responsibility for this maltreatment also implicates the accused as Camp Director, even if he himself did not hit anyone then,* it says at one point in the justification of the verdict, and we ought at least to expect that now there will be a thorough explanation of why the court isn't disposed to follow this convincing legal view of the Public Prosecutor. Instead, there is merely the comment that it's not possible to prove that the Camp Boss ordered each individual act of maltreatment to be inflicted by different guards, as if that carried particular weight.

Congratulations. Mr. Staudinger has truly used clever tactics. Today we are also cleverer; various academic studies about the code of practice of the People's Courts have in the meantime proven in fact that the sentences in the case of guilty verdicts for comparable offenses became milder from year to year. *From 1949 on the emphasis of the verdicts shifted to sentences of a maximum of one year.* So it was downright clever to elude an early trial by fleeing, but also downright clever to face up to it, manfully, in more comfortable times. Lady Luck hasn't yet completely poured out her horn of plenty over August: for, of all people, the Camp Commandant in person, use is made of the extraordinary right to mitigation: the few admitted boxes on the ears are, for this purpose, interpreted as a partial confession; no negative character reference is allowed; the care obligation and war injuries are emphasized. That makes in total, let's say, two and a half years. That is (what an amazing coincidence!) exactly as long as the previous imprisonment in the Third Reich, in the Allied internment camp, and in the Regional Court in Linz. As early as the second of April 1952, August Staudinger is again sleeping in his own bed at home.

Alois Rosenbichler on his cell pallet doesn't know at the outset whether he should be angry or pleased about this outcome of the trial of his former superior. After lengthy consideration, he decides on the latter. In his next handwritten letter to the People's Court asking for clemency, he compares the two verdicts, *and I am indeed not wrong in the assumption that the light sentence can be attributed both to the fact that, apart from less serious personal incrimination, in 1952, after a longish period had elapsed, there was a somewhat more lenient attitude towards our actions.* Nicely formulated is that and well observed, but Mr. Rosenbichler still has to exercise patience a bit longer.

At this time, Michael Kaltenberger is likewise writing a letter that's extremely important for him. The People's Court has finally worked its way up to him and set a date for the start of his trial. The present mayor reads out the renewed request of his predecessor for an impeccable character reference and formally opens the debate in the district committee. We hear: *If Kaltenberger did not always bring up the same old story and were finally to be quiet, everything would already be forgotten,* says the first discussant with noticeable reluctance, after an embarrassing minute of general silence. *None of the political parties bear him any grudges, but he must exhibit appropriate behavior.* Kaltenberger should, in the name of God, get his exonerating piece of paper, but we note at the beginning as a precaution that according to a wise compromise proposal, agreed with three abstentions, it may only be presented at the People's Court: nothing detrimental is recorded in the district offices in St. Pantaleon; Michael Kaltenberger enjoys a good reputation.

Counselor Hiebler and all the other members of the district committee were also of the opinion that the matter should finally be let rest. It is therefore not at all remarkable that Counselor Karl Hiebler, illegal since 1932, and, with a short interruption, an important member of the District Parliament after the National Socialists took over power in 1938, finally wants to be relieved of the burden of the past. Finally, the People's Court agrees to put him next to Michael Kaltenberger in the dock. Hiebler and the other old comrades would indeed easily have had a chance to declare themselves biased, according to the district regulations, and leave the room for this one item on the agenda, as happens time and time again. But the limit to their sense of shame doesn't even stretch that far.

Anyway, people like Michael Kaltenberger who don't recognize the signs of the new era and are still hanging on unembarrassed to yesterday's values are abhorrent to someone like Karl Hiebler. He's carved from different wood in that respect; his gaze firmly focused on a better, rosy future. Soon he'll therefore be able to allow himself, as a reward, to be addressed as Honorable Deputy Mayor. *For submission to the People's Court*, the disstrict also gives Karl Hiebler an endorsement which says: *In the last District Council elections Mr. Karl Hiebler was elected to the District Council and to be parliamentary party leader of the SPÖ, and, on account of his loyal conduct towards his fellow men, he is very highly thought of and popular.* A similar document about Hiebler's character, issued exactly five years ago by the same St. Pantaleon district for the same People's Court, has a slightly different emphasis: *fickle and very cunning. Does not enjoy any particular popularity.* That was admittedly at the time when Karl had to take a short, strategic, compulsory break as local politician and could mutate in peace and quiet from National Socialist to Socialist.

The Chamber of Physicians recently pointed out to its esteemed colleague Dr. Alois Straffner from the Black half of the Reich, that the pension contributions for district physicians should, according to contract, long since have been taken over by the local authorities. Straffner has overlooked that and now imagines that these sums will be charged going back three years to Haigermoos district, but St. Pantaleon will be completely spared further payments, and the prescribed levels of contribution will be required only from the present. Furthermore, the dear doctor generously donates the monies from Haigermoos to St. Pantaleon for the new war memorial because something's brewing there.

In May of 1953, Michael Kaltenberger is sentenced by the People's Court. The camps in Weyer are not an issue at any point, neither in the questioning nor in the trial. However, the accused, Kaltenberger, is in any case found guilty of denunciation and furthermore of mortification and affront to human dignity owing to a particularly reprehensible attitude, as well as illegal activity for the NSDAP between 1933 and 1938. The light sentence of only two years in prison is because of exceptional mitigating grounds: no previous convictions, the obligation to care for his innocent family, and his good reputation that the district attested to afresh exactly three days ago. The sentence counts as served.

Karl Hiebler's acquittal results from the absence of

hard proof. The accused may well in his time have repeatedly mentioned to SA people and unknown civilians subversive statements made by citizens of the village, but it could no longer be conclusively determined who in the end actually reported the people concerned. His illegal NS activities before the *Anschluss* would only have been evaluated in connection with a conviction on the other counts.

At the start of 1954, Victim Welfare has to deal with a curious case. Somebody evidently wishes to apply for government support and claims, in connection with a Gypsy Camp in Weyer, district: St. Pantaleon, to have lost close relatives in the NS period. Through a series of relevant solicitations, the experts are now indeed aware of the District Labor Education Camp in the same place, but nobody has ever heard anything about a Gypsy Camp. So an inquiry is made in writing to the Federal Police Headquarters in Linz.

Yes, something like that did exist. They know that. We don't want to raise any objections to this correct information but rather to the further pertinent police remarks. Namely, the questioner is initially told about the relevant Gypsy Decree from the Reich Security Main Office. *But since the Gypsies did not observe regulations and kept leaving their district of residence, Gypsy Camps had to be established.* We thus note that on closer inspection the victims are once again the real perpetrators and vice versa; in the end, the troublesome Romanies manifestly owe their internment in fact not to National Socialist racial delusion but to the breaking of laws that apply to everyone or, let's be more precise, to some people. At any rate, the instructions of the Director General for public security regarding the Gypsy menace are studied closely, and the exemplary phrasing of the highest policeman in the land is properly used.

Furthermore, to our great surprise, we learn directly from the Upper Austrian Headquarters of the custodians of order that the institution run by an assistant detective from the Linz Criminal Police only existed a total of a very few weeks: *The Gypsy Camp established on January 19, 1941, was dissolved on March 2, 1941.*

Anyone, who as a Sinto or Romany painstakingly reconstructs the suffering of his family, collects material, and claims entitlement to benefits under the Victim Welfare Law, not only has little chance of success because the Gypsies were still second-class citizens after 1945 and are not put on a par with other victim groups, at least formally, until 1988, but above all because the Republic of Austria has not the slightest wish to reconstruct even superficially the genocide of the Romanies. Thirteen years after these past events, such absurd official disclosures are possible at any time; so the person concerned can be told to his face that six weeks for father and mother in a camp were not really worth mentioning.

If anybody refuses point blank to be turned away and now asks in court the irritating question about what in the opinion of the Federal Police Headquarters in Linz then happened to those people who were interned for such a short time and why they all, without exception, are now missing, the answer is the famous shrug of the shoulders: they were merely transferred to Lackenbach in Burgenland. *What happened there to the Gypsies is not known.* On the other hand, it's not only the Ministry of the Interior which has been warning its officials for a long time about ominous hordes of Gypsies about to stream in from the east *claiming racial or political persecution*, when they, at the time, had merely been subjected to certain measures taken on account of their asocial way of life.

It's really in vogue that people should remain calm, that

people should not bear grudges, that even deeply involved, extremely highly educated, influential, and almost financially independent villagers like Dr. Alois Straffner profess their radical belief in a culture of selective memory and do all in their power to promote that. The court files that have just been closed remain inaccessible for decades to come. As for what's not on memorial plaques, what's in missing or destroyed documents, what the victims or their relatives try in desperation to prove, as for which state authorities give false information after just a few years, this matter is gradually disintegrating, is beginning to have never existed. *Allegedly* is the term used from now on, or *It is claimed that*. Anyone who tells the truth runs the danger of being outlawed, and the very vehemence with which disrespectful recollection is fought off speaks volumes.

In St. Pantaleon, they're not really having a lot of luck with their new heroes' memorial, a state of affairs which mirrors the makeshift way that values were cobbled together in the postwar world. For some time now, there has been agitated talk about whether it's really acceptable that the soldier depicted falling in battle may indeed soon fall from his pedestal. He's only four years old, and already rust is emerging from all his pores. Whatever material sculptor Pacher may have used, it wasn't at any rate what was ordered and paid for. They'd probably win a court case, but for the community council members it's another matter whether the artist under suspicion could afford to pay the costs of the repair and the legal proceedings. So instead an assessor is brought in, legally bound by oath, who painstakingly itemizes the damage. For the time being, the district pays for the repair work, but at the same time makes claims for compensation. Opinions differ about the prospects of a successful outcome.

Meanwhile, Alois Rosenbichler has hired a new attorney, and the new one immediately approaches the

Federal President once again. The web of legends around his client's life is depicted on five pages, in more detail than ever before, enriched by heartrending details which weren't known up to now: a severe wound suffered by the man once dismissed from the *Wehrmacht* because of stomach complaints has now made him into a pitiable wounded warrior, before he, particularly short-tempered on account probably of the consequences of the injuries, was to become a guard in Weyer. It's also hard to deny a certain charm to the fairytale dished up for the first time about his immediate appointment to a military criminal division after the original proceedings were halted in 1942. This, however, seems not to have occurred to the medical orderly in the Ranshofen aluminum works until many years later.

On closer examination, the dialectically trained lawyer unobtrusively suggests to the Honorable Federal President that this should even be counted as a mitigating circumstance for the notorious liar Rosenbichler. His stubborn plea of not guilty in the trial is in fact due to a natural urge for self-preservation and an instinctive sense of shame. In addition, it is *an experience observed repeatedly, particularly after 1945, that the accused unloaded a part of their guilt onto an absent fellow criminal whom they perhaps thought was dead in order to exonerate themselves.* Now poor Alois has, however, popped up again unexpectedly after years abroad, and to make matters worse, at a time when the proceedings against the other SA men had long since begun. As a consequence, the assumption was at least not to be summarily dismissed. Finally, Dr. Oskar Welz takes the liberty *to submit the request that the case of Alois Rosenbichler, which was certainly merely a product of the situation at that time,* be judged worthy of the requested clemency. But that doesn't happen.

We might almost be inclined to take the nice phrase about the mere "product of the situation at that time" as an occasion to make a few short closing remarks. But Alois Rosenbichler has been a man of action since time immemorial, and soon he will by mistake commit an act that contributes perhaps substantially more than a thousand words to bringing the longed-for freedom to the mere thirty-five year old. So we will not return to the mere product until later.

Prisoners' home, Garsten near Steyr, May 1954: Alois Rosenbichler is working as industriously as ever in the institution's market garden. Because of inattentiveness, though, a seemingly stupid misfortune befalls him today. He injures his left index finger so badly that the top third has to be amputated. Yet, on the other hand, the unfortunate man can now point out to the People's Court in a further bid for clemency arguing that he *suffered greatly both spiritually and physically. And did so especially when in May of this year I had an accident on the job, in which I lost the index finger of my left hand.*

The Republic of Austria is finally getting back to normal. The year 1955 has begun; the four occupying powers will leave this year; the signing of the state treaty is imminent; perpetual neutrality is on the agenda, people will keep their opinions to themselves and let the others talk, as a national poet to whom people should have listened said long ago. On the twenty-eighth of April, it's imperative to celebrate ten years of the Second Republic fittingly. To mark this, a generous amnesty is planned for eligible criminals. A bid for clemency is composed for Alois Rosenbichler. With reference to his last application, it says there that the candidate justifies his request primarily with the fact that he has served half his sentence, and *thereby atoned sufficiently, especially since he lost his left index finger in a work-related accident in May of 1954. The Public Prosecutor's Office in Linz does not consent to the request for clemency. The People's Court approves the petition for clemency to mark the ten *years since the liberation of the Republic of Austria.*

He should just go home then, should Alois; we're happy not to have to have anything more to do with this man. Let us just finally put it on record that the amputation of part of his left index finger has, in accordance with the seemingly atavistic discretion of the court, thus actually substantially reduced and successfully concluded his atonement. In memory of the liberation from the yoke of National Socialism, that very Austria, for which he only had contempt for so long, presents him with the last seven short years of what we believe was his already modest sentence.

To celebrate the day, on the spring morning when the prison gates open for Alois Rosenbichler and countless other pardoned men, the Austrian Minister of Education appeals to the country's young people in a broadcast to schools transmitted by all the radio stations. The liberation from the yoke of National Socialism is, admittedly, not on the tip of his tongue; that kind of language is not appropriate for Dr. Heinrich Drimmel. He will be able to speak for a solid half hour without coming up against words like "liberation" or "National Socialism" in his manuscript. We all make an effort to follow him, but we simply can't manage to work out what indeed led to those ruins out of which the country rose anew amid sacrifices. Exactly ten years have passed since *those days of confused events*, when *the remorseless modern mechanized war came to an end*, says the Minister vaguely, but in concrete terms he evokes the *image of our poor tormented country, as it looked in the year 1945*. "Poor" and "tormented" do not stimulate any further associations; instead, there's extensive talk of the Austrian miracle of reconstruction and new construction, and this decade was, furthermore, unquestionably a heroic age for women. We thus make edifying discoveries about the bravery of a mother's heart, ditto about the fatherland, united right down to the ramparts of the Karavanke mountains in the south. The ancient civilized nation was not only feeding on ancient times, but was already looking to the future again; *while social and political unrest was shaking the foundations of the nations on all the continents, the people and the government in Austria set all the nations of the whole world an example of how to live and work together in peace.*

Merely a product of the situation at that time, that's what the case of Alois Rosenbichler is for his competent lawyer, probably just as all the concentration camps and work camps were merely products of the confusion of the events of the situation at that time. We're all jettisoned is the message, flotsam on the sea of time, and when it gets stormy we just have to cling tighter to the ships' planks, close ranks tighter, and put our feet down more firmly than usual on other people – laws of nature. Individual guilt pales in this pseudo-philosophical scenario. Social responsibility? What a ludicrous thought.

What's the point please of having a purely academic discussion, people like us are told, if all of that is in effect not true at all any longer? The waves have long since been smoothed out; meanwhile, the significant currents in the nation's world-views move on brilliantly; in their joint efforts, they lay the past to rest, out of a sense of responsibility for the future. *Through truth and justice / To moderation and order / With morals and laws! / United, united / In love and loyalty / To you, my Austria!*

Had we ourselves experienced and participated in these fifteen years and not merely watched and made notes, without attracting any notice, who knows how we might have behaved. Would we have been more cowardly than was necessary, more courageous than was sensible? Would we finally find ourselves now in 1955, the year of jubilation, among the small group of people watched by distrusting eyes, sitting, for instance, at the regulars' table in Kaltenberger's pub in the village center of St. Pantaleon, who, in the face of the grotesque self-stylization of Austria as the strong heart of the globe and model for the rest of the world, unflinchingly supports the demand for humble contrition and acknowledges joint responsibility for the unprecedented barbarity of the most recent past? This would be mere idle speculation.

We assume we have the right to examine things so closely that it hurts, not because we think we know it all or because we might be unaccustomed to self-doubt. To tell the truth, some time ago we received a visitor unexpectedly; it may well have been that it was late at night. So what answer would you give to a girl who was murdered back then at the age of nine years, if she's suddenly standing there and begging you to take her life? How do you imagine that? was what we gave her to ponder when she finally finished telling her story. It is not so simple; we'd have to make a massive effort to satisfy your wish. That would be an awful lot of work. But she wouldn't be dissuaded. That's how it is when children have once got something into their heads.

We reckon for the little girl that it will take, at a rough estimate, a good two hundred pages until we can, in the middle of the fifties, enter the pretty, slightly run-down inner courtyard of Wildshut Castle in St. Pantaleon. We're guided by the signs with the federal eagle, find the correct entrance straight away, slip unnoticed past the lady in the outer office, who, among other things, is responsible for arranging appointments with the District Judge, and there we are already, standing on the parquet floor of his office. There is no pressing business and the judge is dutifully sorting portfolios that have been set aside. He's working on some rather dusty foster-care files today. As we appear, he's untying, without haste, the knot in a frayed piece of string, and opening the battered wrapper on one massive bundle. With a soft red crayon, the Honorable Regional Court Judge writes the notation *of age* on the top left of the first yellowed sheet because the expected death certificate of the former ward is not attached. It doesn't irritate him at all that the most recent procedure in the file was recorded in May of 1941. At that time, the underage Amalia Blach, born on the third of June 1932, was assigned to an official legal guardian from the department in Wildshut in nearby Ostermiething. The girl's address was Weyer No. 6.

In the spring of 1955, the conviction grows in my parents that they want to bring children into the new, free Austria with its promising future, and I grow in my mother's womb. Shortly before Christmas, I then enter the world and grow up in a country blessed by the economic miracle which nobody wants to injure, possibly out of an instinctive sense of shame. And so they miss the opportunity, after successfully treating the root of all evil, to be able to feel for once what it really means to be free of pain. Everywhere there's hustle and bustle; nobody seems any longer to notice the long white arrows on the grey house walls that a few years earlier pointed to the air raid shelters. They still point diagonally downwards, at the eye level of a child my size. I quickly order all this in my own mind; I am, after all, moving on the carefully smoothed, thin crusts of a mysterious new eruption, about whose dangers these arrows to the underworld are a haunting warning to me. I also note the last ruins of the war: broad, open, grassless, leveled, rubble surfaces near the city center, on which the heat flickers in midsummer, with isolated wooden barracks on them, which appear unnaturally superimposed on this environment and accommodate a school. And the tattered photo album belonging to my father, who died young, is also a warning to me, with its picture of the boisterous company carnival celebrations next to one of a hanged Tito partisan and with the respective captions for the pictures. No, I'm a long way from assuming firm ground under my feet, and at a remarkably early age, I am quite surprised it doesn't simply give way under me, am surprised that it doesn't give way under all of us and we perish unawares.

Author's Note

This text should not be understood as a work of nonfiction. Nevertheless, historical authenticity is a particular concern of my prose narrative since matters nobody had to invent are still all too readily dismissed as pure fiction. Many names, particularly those of the criminals and informers, have been altered, except for those of high-ranking district and Reich-level NS functionaries. This was done out of consideration for the descendants. Orthographic variations of the proper names in the passages taken verbatim from documents were also retained, as were stylistic oddities and obvious errors.

Quotations taken from original documents are in italics and are part of the aesthetic concept of this novel. They are not intended in any way to invite people to study the files, but they do serve, in their fragmentary character, as intensification. They're not comparable to quotations in academic studies. For this reason, I have not followed the academic format and content myself with expressing my thanks to those institutions, archives, and individuals who made possible this undertaking, which initially seemed very unpromising.

The book is not based on oral history sources written down decades after the fact, recalled in the fuzziness of human memory and personal bias, but rather on a few thousand pages from original files dating from the years 1940 to 1955, with their countless cross-references. Among them are notes taken during hearings; minutes from interrogations of witnesses, which to a large extent tally with one another, and interrogations of accused parties; all sorts of correspondence between authorities, memos, applications, and letters of complaint; as well as statistical material from budgets, registry office documents, priests' burial lists, etc. There is not room here to thank everyone, but I would particularly like to thank the Upper Austrian Regional Archives, the Documentation Archives of the Austrian Resistance, the Cultural Organization of Austrian Romanies, and the Ebensee Concentration Camp Memorial Site.

In the year 1999, the war memorial in St. Pantaleon was rebuilt from scratch, in a fashion true to the original. On the occasion of the second dedication celebrated in front of the mortally wounded soldier in his renovated splendor, the commemorative speech of Pumberger, Freedom Party Member of the National Parliament, culminated in the following thought-provoking words: *Our ancestors also defended our country, And they really showed their whole commitment to the cause and knew what they were fighting for. And that is why it will always be our task and duty to express our hearty thanks to all of those who had to sacrifice their youth in the battle for our fatherland in both World Wars, particularly in the Second World War. Because it was they who preserved our country for us.*

Almost twelve months later, the district of St. Pantaleon set up a memorial site beside the river Moosach in June of 2000 for the victims of both camps in Weyer. This followed from a suggestion by citizens, men and women, who thought that it wasn't right simply to suppress in perpetuity a dark chapter of contemporary history. Since then, there has been a dedicated place where people can think of those who met a violent death here in the village and those children born in St. Pantaleon who were bestially murdered only a few months later in Lodz and Chelmno.

At the same time, the original names of people the readers encounter in this book are surfacing again as pseudonyms in certain right-wing internet discussion forums. Thus on July 22, 2000, at 3:43, for example, an internet chatter called "Michael Kaltenberger/Gau Oberdonau" complains about the lack of solidarity between Reich Germans loyal to the nation, and (ethnic) *Volksgenossen* from the Ostmark and South Tyrol in their ethnic struggle.

Author's Postsript

Since this book appeared in the year 2001, I have received (quite apart from the usual mail from readers) over a hundred letters, e-mails, and phone calls from various corners of Austria, in which further light is thrown on the events on which my novel is based. Elderly people, themselves actually witnesses or directly affected, got in touch, just as did younger people, whose relatives were involved as victims or perpetrators. Even descendants of contemporaries who suddenly, without having actively done anything, saw themselves tangled up in some way or other in the murderous deeds evidently felt the need to put their knowledge at my disposal.

In an epistle stretching to pages, for example, the son of the then district doctor from a neighboring village tells me that his father was called out in the autumn of 1940 in the middle of the night.. A guard from Weyer in an SA uniform apologized politely and "only" desired signatures for mortuary remains; the duty camp doctor was in fact momentarily unavailable. Would the honorable doctor please enter pneumonia on the forms that had been brought along? Dr. H. resolutely refused to sign without a thorough examination of the dead. That would be out of the question, the SA man replied; strangers were forbidden on principle to enter the camp grounds. After a heated debate, the doctor, who had long since been informed by railway employees in the resistance movement about the conditions at the camp, swung himself onto his motorcycle and drove to St. Pantaleon. He finally did manage to get a look at the corpses. On account of the clearly visible injuries, Dr. H. was of the firm opinion that he had to assume that a third party was to blame and compiled a report.

He should remember that his young wife had recently died, was what he was then told; he had four children, the youngest one year old. Could he take responsibility for the Gestapo picking him up the next day and ordering him to the front again in another few days? Towards daybreak, the son writes, his father signed. In 1977, the year of his death, the aged Dr. H. then told him *in a state of great emotional arousal* the events of that night which still continued to haunt him in his dreams. The son now carried this knowledge with him without being able to do anything with it since the St. Pantaleon-Weyer camp seemed never to have existed. Twenty-five years later, Mr. H. read *Heart Flesh Degeneration* and says in conclusion that this book finally put his mind at rest.

A second story: On the day after the broadcast on Austrian Television of the TV documentary with the same name as my book, there was a ring at the door of a survivor of the work education camp whose misdemeanor as an eighteen year old had consisted in being absent from the Hitler Youth one Sunday without permission. Outside, with a large bunch of roses, stands the step-daughter of one of the principal perpetrators. It turns out by coincidence that today both are living only a few hundred meters apart. She saw him yesterday in the television film in the torture cellar of the former camp, describing the sadism of the guards. She had only a vague idea of what role her stepfather had played in the camp, and of course she had been completely unaware that Mr. H. was one of the victims. Now she just felt a spontaneous need to bring him these flowers, that was all. Yes, so do please come in, says the wife of the perplexed man of the house; the people converse for two hours; tears of release and relief flow on both sides.

Even after my readings all around the country, the picture is this: If it's desired, a man with a soft voice says, he would be happy to tell the audience the reason for the admission of his uncle Josef Mayer, whose story of suffering occupies a large amount of space in my book, right up to his death by torture. In front of an audience of over 130 people, the man, who is certainly not accustomed to performances of this type, describes in great detail how the soldier from the front comes home unexpectedly on Christmas leave, encounters his wife in bed with the NS mayor of the small town, a mere twenty kilometers from Braunau, and how, understandably upset, the man throws him out, and he's collected by the Gestapo the very next morning and admitted to the camp for asocials. After all, mayors did have the inalienable right to dispose in this elegant manner of people they wanted to be rid of. And the nephew tells how he had to find out from my novel how the uncle was tortured to death and buried in St. Pantaelon cemetery without a proper grave. I can provide for the nephew all Josef Mayer's original documents; birth, marriage, and death certificates are stored up to now in the attic of the St. Pantaleon district office. Nobody ever made the effort to look for relatives, give further aid, clear things up.

Attorney General Dr. Neuwirth apparently attempted in vain in 1941 to throw light onto the darkness around the admission of Josef Mayer, whose violent death set the ball rolling for the whole affair. In the files, there's only one single short witness statement, according to which Mayer, when asked by a guard shortly after being admitted why he was there, answered, *because of my wife*. The information given by the nephew sixty years later exactly fit this comment, which I had previously not been able to fathom.

In a vocational college a seventeen-year-old girl, an

apprentice hairdresser, spoke up and reported how moved she was by what she just heard. The teachers had hardly briefed them at all before my reading, thus the surprise was all the greater. Her great-grandma, the young woman recounts, in perhaps somewhat less elaborate words, was herself a Sintiza, that is, a Gypsy. Right up to the present day, the old lady had been suffering from two things in particular: First, from the loss of almost her entire family, which was murdered by the Nazis, and secondly from the fact that after the war nobody had ever been interested in this story, and that the genocide of the Upper Austrian Sinti, who had been verifiably recorded in the district at least since the time of Maria Theresia, had never happened as far as the general public was concerned. And she too, the great-granddaughter, had never once in her whole life heard anything about it, except from her great-grandmother, until I read aloud now and recounted how it all happened. This girl is not shy either in front of over a hundred people from various social classes and finds very vivid words, which have a strong impact on the young people.

I get to know other relatives of murdered Roma and Sinti, am able to tell them for the first time about what became of their cousins. For example, the woman who was pregnant when interned gave birth to her child in the camp – when exactly it came into the world, what it was called, and where its trail ends. Friendships develop; I finally make the proposal to three women in one of these Sinti families, born in 1923, 1946, and 1976, that they write down their life stories, which are eventful. In autumn, 2004, the book I edited, *Uns hat es nicht geben sollen* [We Should Not Have Existed], is published, with numerous illustrations and documents, the first sizeable publication by an old, established Upper Austrian minority group.

In southern Bohemia, without having to look for long,

I come upon Ludwig Steffel's well-cared-for grave. The man who they searched for after the war in the wrong Kirchschlag as a witness in the People's Court trial only survived the punishments by torture in St. Pantaleon-Weyer for a short period; in April 1942, his lingering illness came to an end. Broken in body and spirit, he returned to Kirchschlag/Svetlik, Gertrude reports. The only open pub in the village was almost empty; only two women were sitting there. I ask if anyone speaks German and whether the neighboring district office would open in the afternoon. In the familiar Mühlviertel dialect, Gertrude asks why. I answer, oh, it's to do with a very old story, about a certain Ludwig Steffel. That's my grandfather, she says, and at first does not know at all what's happening to her.

From all directions, the pieces of the jigsaw puzzle supplied to me pile up; there is not one that can't find its place in the framework of that reality I'd studied in the documents and which I had formed into a piece of literature which now stands on its own. For example, a German lecturer informs me that in the estate of Georg Rendl, a fellow author from the middle of the last century, whose works once were published by Insel Verlag and who lived from 1938 till 1972 near the boundary of St. Pantaleon, there are war letters, sent him by his wife, which repeatedly refer to the camp in Weyer. She reports on one occasion early in 1941 about a twenty-year-old who had no idea at all that he was a Gypsy until he was interned there. His family led an assimilated life in Steyr; until his arrest, he himself worked there in a munitions factory; three sisters were married to soldiers at the front. It was only in the camp that he came into contact with the customs, habits, and language of the Gypsies.

Less than a fortnight later, Bertha Rendl reports the troubles of the camp doctor; indeed, Egyptian pneumonia had broken out in the camp; twenty Gypsies had become infected. That is precisely at the time when the first cases of death in the second camp occur, including that of the five-year-old Maria Daniel who dies officially of heart failure, but according to the notes of the Medical Officer dies of croupous pneumonia.

Even after the war, there is no literary text by Georg Rendl himself (who not only sets his great industrial novel *The Glass-Blowers of Bürmoos* in that region) or any other sort of written record by him relating to the two Reich District Camps right on his doorstep, although he was very well acquainted with the Camp Doctor.

Furthermore, the affluent doctor is also indirectly linked to a second, far more prominent writer. As early as the summer of 1937, as Gert Kerschbaumer reports in his book *Stefan Zweig: The Flying Salzburger*, the soon-to-be NS dignitary rents out his house in the Salzburg district of Nonntal to the family of the Jew Stefan Zweig, who was already exposed to strong attacks and who admittedly does not, however, move in there himself in the end. His wife Friderike, on the other hand, spends the "last months of Austria" with her daughters "in the charming house," which guests of the family like Joseph Roth enjoy visiting (Friderike Zweig in *Reflections*). The Zweig angle enhances once more the ambiguous personality of this central figure in my novel.

Ludwig Laher

AFTERWORD
HISTORICAL BACKGROUND
by
Florian Schwanninger

On March 12, 1938, German troops invaded Austria. This marked a caesura in the history of Austria and had such unprecedented cataclysmic and devastating effects that its reverberations are still being felt today, more than sixty years after the end of the Nazi regime, and are still very much a subject of public debate. Just as the collapse of the Danube monarchy and the founding of the Republic in 1918 made a deep mark in the country's history, so the consequences of the *Anschluss* (Annexation) to the Third Reich twenty years later were to shape the political, social, and economic development of Austria for decades. To this day, their importance should not be underestimated.

When Hitler ordered the 8th Army to occupy neighboring Austria, he destroyed any hopes of victory the pro-Austrian camp might have had in the referendum set for March 13 by Chancellor Schuschnigg to decide the future of the Republic. At the same time as 65,000 members of the German Army crossed the border, many local National Socialists and sympathizers who already held positions at various levels in the fallen *Ständestaat* (Austrian Corporate State) took over power.[1] This power was taken over "from

---

[1] In 1933 the parliament was dissolved by Christian-Social Chancellor Engelbert Dollfuß. Furthermore, he banned both the Nazi and the Communist Parties. After the uprising of the Social Democratic Security League in February 1934, the government also banned all organizations of the Workers' Movement and the Social Democrats and relied as a result on the Patriotic Front, a Unified Party along Italian lines.

the grassroots" by means of street demonstrations of a threatening nature, public marches by previously banned party groupings, and symbolic activities.

Although Austria had not had a democratic political system since the year 1933 and was under authoritarian rule, oppression and persecution reached a qualitatively new and previously unknown level after the annexation to the Third Reich in March 1938. In came not only the German troops but also the Gestapo, the Security Service of the Reich High Command, and other divisions of the National Socialist regime of terror. At the same time, the formerly illegal Austrian National Socialists used their newly acquired positions of power to proceed ruthlessly against their political opponents and the Jewish population and also to settle their old accounts from the period 1933-1938 when they were banned during the Austro-Fascist *Ständestaat*.

Immediately after the German invasion, about 70,000 people (out of 7 million inhabitants) were put in prisons or concentration camps for lesser or greater periods of time. On the one hand, there were intimidation campaigns of limited duration; on the other, however, the Austrian Nazis removed political opponents indefinitely or even killed them. Former high-ranking officials in the defunct *Ständestaat*, adherents of the Catholic-Conservative party, members of illegal socialist or communist groups, and countless Jews were among the first victims of these waves of arrests. Many people never returned from custody, and for many of those arrested, the gates of the prisons and camps did not open to release them until May 1945.

At this point, it is important to highlight the wave of suicides of those desperate citizens who were affected by the Nuremberg Race Laws. The only way that many Austrian men and women could evade persecution by the new rulers was to seek refuge abroad. After democracy came to an end in 1933/34, thousands of members of the now illegal Austrian Workers' Movement were already living in exile, where they organized resistance, first against the *Ständestaat* and, after 1938, against Nazi rule. More than 1,400 Austrians, for example, fought as volunteers in the Spanish Civil War on the side of the Republic against the Franco Regime.

After this first wave of terror had swept over the country, the Nazi regime, led by German advisors and party functionaries, turned the referendum into an elaborately staged propaganda campaign. No element of propaganda was left to chance, and the National Socialists could draw on the support of wide sections of the population which were hard hit by high unemployment and poverty. The result of the referendum about the annexation of Austria was a resounding 99% in favor. In various ways the combination of terror, intimidation, promises, propaganda, enthusiasm, and almost perfect organization had secured this result. Furthermore, 300,000 to 400,000 Austrians, particularly Jews and persons who were politically suspect, were barred from participating in the referendum.

In the process of establishing the Nazi regime in the newly formed "Ostmark" (Eastern territory) or "Alpine and Danube Districts," as the area formerly known as Austria was now called, National Socialist Third Reich legislation relating to the suppression and persecution of political opponents and other alien groups was implemented within a relatively short period of time. Almost overnight, the Jewish population and those persons falling under the Nuremberg Laws lost all their rights and consequently their property. Right after the invasion there had been cases of unofficial "Aryanization" in the form of looting, for example, and there had also been numerous cases of physical attacks. This wave of violence increased to a previously unheard of extent during the "Reichskristallnacht" (The Night of Broken Glass) in November of 1938. The National Socialists' radical anti-Semitism fell on very fertile ground in large sections of the Austrian population and developed its destructive momentum fuelled by personal greed and hardening attitudes. After civil and property rights were annulled, the final stage was deportation to death camps in Eastern Europe. Even in rural areas like the Braunau district, where there were very few known Jews, the Aryanization measures were carried out in full, and the victims were threatened and constantly bullied. Towards the end of the war, Jews of "mixed blood" and Jewish spouses in so-called "mixed marriages" with "Aryans" were finally also threatened with being sent to a concentration camp. For most, the only escape was to go into hiding.

The full extent of the Nazi reign of terror was to be seen not only in the death camps of Eastern Europe. Some of the most gruesome sites of murder were right in the heart of Upper Austria, which was then known as "Upper Danube," the "Homeland of the Führer." In this region alone, there were more than thirty concentration camps of varying sizes. The most prominent of these camps was in Mauthausen near the Danube, some twenty kilometers east of Linz. In Mauthausen and its numerous satellite camps, which spread like a net over the whole length and breadth of the region, more than 100,000 people perished in the SS "Destruction through Labor" campaign. The largest killing center of the Nazi euthanasia campaign was located in Hartheim Castle near Eferding, in the vicinity of Linz, the town which was envisaged as the "Führer's retreat in his old age." It was in this old Renaissance castle that more than 18,000 handicapped, mentally ill, and socially misfit were killed by poison gas under the auspices of the T4 Campaign of 1940-41. This was followed by the 14f13 Campaign of 1941-44, which resulted in the murder of almost 10,000 prisoners from Dachau and Mauthausen who were unfit for work, sick, or disabled.

National Socialist Persecution in the Upper Danube District also had an extremely high impact outside the aforementioned concentration camps and killing centers. Numerous fanatical Nazi functionaries wanted to single out the "Home District of the Führer" for particularly tight enforcement of strict measures to combat and eliminate political opponents, "racial inferiors" and "national pests." The following passage, for example, is found in a directive from the Braunau/Inn Regional Government on "Combating the Gypsy Nuisance": "It is the wish of the Regional Nazi Party Leader to make the Führer's Home District free of Gypsies, and all efforts must therefore be made to achieve this goal quickly."[2] As Laher's novel clearly shows, the Upper Austrian Sinti and Roma had been subject to discrimination for a long period, and from the beginning of the Nazi regime, they were brutally persecuted and finally almost entirely eradicated. Under Nazi rule, the Sinti and Roma, who were referred to by the negatively charged term "Zigeuner," were, like the Jews, first deprived of their rights, then forced to remain wherever they were residing at the time, and finally transported to assembly camps. It was from these camps, where a substantial number of the prisoners perished on account of the atrocious living conditions, that survivors were taken to the concentration camps when the industrial mass killings began. Only a few Upper Austrian Sinti and Roma survived these murder campaigns. After 1945 they were, furthermore, not recognized as victims of National Socialism on account of continued prejudice, and most had to wait until the 1990s for compensation for the injustice they had suffered.

In the Upper Danube District, the particular zeal of

---

[2] Braunau/Inn Regional Government, Zl. 18/IV-39, *Combating the Gypsy Nuisance*, in Laher Archive, St. Pantaleon.

the regional and local authorities can also be observed in the relationship between the Nazi regime and the Catholic Church. In no other district of the Ostmark of comparable size were so many priests arrested and put in prisons and concentration camps as in Upper Danube. Within the Führer's Home Region, the Region of Braunau on the river Inn (which reverted in 1945 to being known as the District of Braunau on the river Inn) was at the top of the list as far as arrests of Catholic priests were concerned. Priests were arrested in about a third of the parishes. In the deanery of Ostermiething, where the parish of St. Pantaleon is to be found, and to which the village of Weyer formerly belonged, as many as two thirds of the parishes suffered from priests being arrested.

If account is taken of the events before and during annexation and of the participation of many Austrians in the Nazi annihilation programs in occupied Europe, the almost sacrosanct Second Republic description of Austria as the "first victim of National Socialism" has only limited validity. This description was certainly true at the level of national legislation because the country was occupied by a foreign power. But people very frequently adopted the comfortable status of "collective Nazi victim," a phrase which goes back to the Moscow Declaration of 1943. The aim was to absolve themselves of any guilt and suppress the fact that a substantial part of the Austrian population had been involved in upholding Nazi rule and carrying out its policy of persecution. It was only in the immediate postwar years that there was public debate about the Allies' demand, made in the aforementioned Moscow Declaration, that Austria itself had to contribute towards liberation from the Nazi regime and that such efforts would be recognized appropriately once the Third Reich was defeated.

When the former National Socialists were reintegrated

and rehabilitated as a consequence of the start of the Cold War, the victims of National Socialism and members of the antifascist resistance movement had less and less influence on political life. ÖVP and SPÖ[3] resistance fighters were marginalized in their parties, and the communists, who had suffered by far the greatest losses in the organized resistance, were excluded from the political arena. In stark contrast, the former National Socialists now represented a significant potential group of voters who were ardently wooed by both major parties. They were in fact seen as useful allies in the fight against the common enemy in the east.

Anti-Semitism did not indeed disappear from people's minds at the end of the Nazi regime. American surveys showed, after 1945, how large the proportion of the population was which was not as antifascist as it had officially claimed to the Allies. Public awareness of the victims of war and fascism was still highly selective. While there was talk in public of crimes and war victims, this generally referred to Allied bombing, army prisoners of war in Allied camps, and the looting and rape by the Russians in the first few weeks after liberation. For a long time, the dominant political powers failed to address the question of National Socialist crimes which took place with the participation of Austrians. It was only in the first years after liberation in 1945 that efforts were made by legal authorities to deal with this period. The initially strong jurisdiction of the specially formed People's Courts became more and more half-hearted as the years went on. After the withdrawal of the Allies following the signing of the State Treaty in 1955, this form of jurisprudence was abolished completely, and an amnesty was granted to many of those who had previously been sentenced. In the following decades, there

---

[3] ÖVP: Österreichische Volkspartei [Austrian People's Party]; SPÖ: Sozialistische Partei Österreichs [Austrian Socialist Party]

were very few court cases dealing with Nazi crimes.
For years, people did not speak of what had happened during the Nazi period. Interestingly, this was true in both the public and the private sphere. This period was very often a taboo topic, not only among the families of people who were involved in the regime and crimes of the National Socialists, but also among the families of the victims. Long after the end of the Nazi regime, various traumatic experiences continued to exert a lasting effect on victims and people who had witnessed crimes, and this made it impossible for them to talk openly about what they themselves had experienced. It often took several decades until people were willing to discuss these events with family or friends. There was a similar reticence in the public sphere in Austria. Here too, it was only from the 1970s onwards, and particularly in the 1980s, that there was a broader debate about the National Socialist period. In the wake of the debate about Austrian President Kurt Waldheim's role in the Nazi period, and as a result of numerous publications, documentaries, and events surrounding the fiftieth anniversary of the German invasion in 1938, a broad cross-section of the public looked afresh at the years 1938-1945.

Florian Schwanninger, born in 1977 in Hochburg/Ach, is an Austrian historian. His volume *Im Heimatkreis des Führers: Nationalsozialismus, Widerstand und Verfolgung im Bezirk Braunau 1938 bis 1945,* Günbach: Steinmassl, 2005 (*In the Homeland of the Führer*) deals comprehensively with National Socialism, resistance, and persecution in the district of Braunau, the area in which Adolf Hitler was born and where both the Nazi camps in Weyer were located.

In 1940 the SA set up a Work Education Camp in St. Pantaleon near Salzburg. After its overhasty closure in 1941, a Gypsy Detention Center was established. Hundreds of arbitrarily incarcerated inmates are tortured there, some murdered. The Camp Doctor is the district doctor who has been called under special circumstances. For a long time he records some harmless cause of death (the "heart flesh degeneration" of a Gypsy woman is, however, not his invention). But one day he calls in the State Attorney's Office. The files relating to the ensuing investigation are extant – after all, it was the Führer in person who cancelled the trial.

For Ludwig Laher the files were the basis of his literary work, which makes use in a sometimes chilling way of the language and logic of the murderers. At the same time he introduces a collective narrator and lets him follow the horrific events once again from the 1940s point of view, and then again from today's viewpoint. Laher also pursues the perpetrators into resurrected Austria and describes the later court proceedings: The judges are mild; in 1955 the principal perpetrator profits from the amnesty to mark the tenth anniversary of the founding of the Second Republic.

The reader who is drawn into the midst of events may well feel his heart miss a beat when he sees how quickly the incursion of bestial conditions into the everyday life of the Austrian provinces becomes normality. And also how quickly everything apparently never happened in that famous zero hour.

The translator, Susan Tebbutt, is Head of German Studies at Mary Immaculate College, University of Limerick, Ireland. She edited the volume *Sinti and Roma: Gypsies in German-Speaking Society and Literature* (Berghahn, 1998) and is co-editor with Nicholas Saul of *The Role of the Romanies: Images and Counter-Images of "Gypsies"/Romanies in European Cultures* (Liverpool University Press, 2004).